Lewis Carroll

Adapted by
Eliza Gatewood Warren

Published by Playmore Inc., Publishers and
Waldman Publishing Corp., New York, New York

ILLUSTRATED CLASSIC EDITIONS

Printed in Canada

Contents

About the Author

As curious, to his biographers, as Alice's adventures was their creator Charles Lutwidge Dodgson (Lewis Carroll), a mid-Victorian who seemed to live two distinct lives.

Born January 27, 1832, in Daresbury, England, Dodgson was the oldest of a clergyman's eleven children and a boy who kept mostly to himself. He entered Oxford in 1851 and joined its mathematics faculty after his graduation— to become, by most accounts, a stuffy if precise teacher, and the author of little-remembered treatises on geometry and symbolic logic. He was also, in 1861, ordained a deacon.

Throughout, Dodgson was exercising more fanciful talents. In 1855, he had written his famous Jabberwocky poem, "'Twas brillig, and the slithy toves...." He drew humorous sketches, still acclaimed, and became one of the century's most outstanding photographers of children. And he wrote, among other startlingly original classics, two adventures of Alice underground, first related aloud for the daughter of his college dean.

Though Dodgson liked children—often presenting little girls with his drawings and photographs—he never married. He died January 14, 1998, in Guildford, England, in his twofold career one of the most unusual men in literature.

She Peeked into the Book.

CHAPTER ONE

Down the Rabbit Hole

One hot summer day as Alice sat idly on the river bank by her sister, she got very tired of having nothing to do. Once or twice she peeked into the book her sister was reading, but it had no pictures or conversation in it, "and what is the use of a book," thought Alice, "without pictures or conversation?"

Just as she was trying to decide (as well as she could, for the hot day made her feel very sleepy) whether or not to get up and pick some daisies to make a daisy chain, a White Rabbit with pink eyes dashed by.

There was nothing so very remarkable in that.

Nor did Alice think it so very unusual to hear the Rabbit say to himself, "Oh, dear! Oh, dear! I shall be late for a very important date."

When she thought about it afterwards, it occurred to her that she ought to have wondered about that, but at the time it all seemed quite natural.

But when the Rabbit actually took a watch out of his waistcoat pocket, looked at it, and then hurried on, Alice jumped to her feet. For she suddenly realized she had never before seen a rabbit with either a waistcoat pocket or a watch to take out of it.

Burning with curiosity, she ran across the field after him, just in time to see him pop down a large rabbit hole under the hedge.

Without a moment's hesitation, Alice jumped in the hole after him, never once considering

The Rabbit Took a Watch Out.

how in the world she would get out again.

The rabbit hole stretched straight ahead like a tunnel for some way, and then dropped off so suddenly that Alice didn't have a moment to think about stopping herself before she fell down a deep well.

Either the well was very deep or she fell slowly, for she had plenty of time as she went down to look about her and to wonder what was going to happen next.

First, Alice tried to look down and make out what she was coming to, but it was too dark to see anything. Then she looked at the sides of the well and noticed that they were filled with cupboards and bookshelves. Here and there maps and pictures hung upon pegs.

She took down a jar from one of the shelves as she passed. It was labeled "Orange Marmalade", but to her great disappointment, it was empty. Alice did not want to drop the jar for fear of killing somebody underneath, so she managed to put it into one of the cupboards as she fell past it.

"Well!" Alice thought to herself. "After a fall like this, I shall think nothing of tumbling downstairs! How brave they'll think me at home! Why I wouldn't say anything about it, even if I fell off the top of the house!"

Down, down, down. Would the fall ever come to an end? "I wonder how many miles I've fallen?" the amazed girl asked aloud. "I must be getting somewhere near the center of the earth. Let me see, that would be four thousand miles down, I think."

Alice had learned several things of this sort at school. Though this was not a very good opportunity to show off her knowledge, as there was no one to listen to her, still it was good practice to repeat it. "But then I wonder what latitude and longitude I've reached," she said.

Now Alice didn't have the slightest idea

Down, Down, Down Alice Fell.

what latitude and longitude were, but she thought they were nice grand words to say.

Presently she began again. "I wonder if I shall fall right through the earth! When I land, I shall have to ask people what is the name of their country. Please, ma'am, is this New Zealand? Or Australia?"

Alice tried to curtsy as she spoke, but can you imagine curtsying as you're falling through the air? Do you think you could manage it?

"What an ignorant little girl she'll think me for asking!" Alice said. "No, it'll never do to ask. Perhaps I shall see it written up somewhere."

Down, down, down Alice fell. There was nothing else to do, so she soon began talking again—this time about her beloved cat, Dinah.

"Dinah will miss me very much tonight, I should think," she cried. "Oh, I hope the family will remember her saucer of milk at tea time. Dinah, my dear, I wish you were here with me! There are no mice in the air, I'm afraid, but you might catch a bat, and that's very much like a mouse, you know. But do cats eat bats, I wonder?"

And here Alice began to get rather sleepy and went on talking to herself in a dreamy sort of way, "Do cats eat bats? Do cats eat bats?" Sometimes she asked, "Do bats eat cats?"

For you see, as she couldn't answer either question, it didn't much matter which way she put it.

She felt that she was dozing off and had just begun to dream that she was walking hand in hand with Dinah and was saying to her very earnestly, "Now, Dinah, tell me the truth— did you ever eat a bat?"

Suddenly Alice went thump, thump, thump and landed in a heap of sticks and dry leaves, and the fall was over.

Alice was not hurt a bit and jumped to her

The Fall Was Over.

feet in a moment. She looked up, but it was all dark overhead. Before her lay another long passage and the White Rabbit was still in sight, hurrying down it.

There was not a moment to be lost. Away flew Alice like the wind, and was just in time to hear him say, as he turned the corner, "Oh my ears and whiskers, how late it's getting!"

She was close behind him when she rounded the corner, but the Rabbit was nowhere in sight. Alice found herself in a long, low hall, which was lit up by a row of lamps hanging from the roof.

There were doors all around the hall, but they were all locked. When Alice had been down one side and up the other, trying every door, she walked sadly down the middle. She couldn't help but wonder how she would ever get out again.

Suddenly Alice came upon a little three legged table, made of solid glass. There was nothing on it but a tiny gold key. Alice's first idea was that this might belong to one of the doors in the hall.

But alas! Either the locks were too large, or the key was too small for them. At any rate, it would not open any of them.

However, on the second time around, she noticed a low curtain she had not seen before. Behind it was a little door about fifteen inches high. She tried the gold key in the lock, and to her delight it fit!

Alice opened the door and found it led into a small passage, not much larger than a rat hole. She knelt down and looked along the passage into the loveliest garden she'd ever seen.

How she longed to get out of that dark hall and wander about among those beds of bright flowers and those cool fountains! But, oh dear, she couldn't even get her head through the doorway.

"Even if my head would go through,"

She Found a Little Bottle.

thought the distraught girl, "it would be of little use without my shoulders. Oh, how I wish I could close up like a telescope. I think I could, if I only knew how to begin."

For so many out-of-the-way things had happened lately, that Alice had begun to think that very few things indeed were really impossible.

There seemed to be no use in waiting by the little door, so she went back to the table, half hoping she might find another key on it, or at any rate a book of rules for closing people up like telescopes.

This time she found a little bottle on it, which certainly was not there before. Around the neck of the bottle was a paper label with the words "DRINK ME" beautifully painted on it in large letters.

It was all very well to say, "Drink me," but Alice was a wise girl and was not going to do that in a hurry.

"No, I'll look first," she said, "and see

whether it's marked 'poison' or not," She had read several nice little stories about children who had been burned and eaten up by wild beasts and other unpleasant things, all because they would not remember the simple rules their friends had taught them.

One was that a red-hot poker will burn you if you hold it too long. Secondly, if you cut your finger very deeply with a knife, it usually bleeds. She had never forgotten that, if you drink much from a bottle marked "poison" it is almost certain to disagree with you sooner or later.

However, this little bottle seemed to be perfectly safe, so Alice ventured to taste it and found it delicious, with a sort of mixed flavor of cherry tart, custard, pineapple, roast turkey, candy, and hot buttered toast. She soon finished it off.

"What a curious feeling," exclaimed Alice. "I must be closing up like a telescope."

That's exactly what happened. She was only

"What a Curious Feeling"

ten inches high, and her face brightened up at the thought that she was now the the right size to go through the little door into that lovely garden.

First, however, she waited for a few minutes to see if she was going to shrink any further. She felt a little nervous about this. "For it might end, you know," Alice said to herself, "in my going out altogether, like a candle. I wonder what I should be like then?"

And she tried to imagine what the flame of a candle looks like after the candle is blown out, for she could not remember ever having seen such a thing.

After awhile, finding that nothing more happened, she decided to go out into the garden. But alas for poor Alice! When she got to the door, she discovered she had forgotten the little gold key. Quickly she returned to the table to get it, but now she found she could not possibly reach it.

Alice could see the key quite plainly through the glass and tried her best to climb up one of the legs of the table, but it was too slippery. When she had tired herself out trying, the poor exhausted child just sat down and cried.

"Come, there's no use in crying like that," Alice lectured herself. "I advise you to stop this minute." She generally gave herself very good advice though she seldom followed it.

Sometimes she scolded herself so severely that she brought tears to her eyes. Once she remembered trying to box her own ears for having cheated herself in a game of croquet she was playing against herself. This curious girl liked to pretend to be two people.

"But it's no use now," Alice thought, "to pretend to be two people. Why, there's hardly enough of me left to make one complete person." Soon she spied a little glass box under the table. She opened it and found a small cake on which the words, "EAT ME" were beauti-

"Well, I'll Eat It."

fully marked in currants.

"Well, I'll eat it," said Alice, "and if it makes me grow larger, I can reach the key. If it makes me grow smaller, I can creep under the door. Either way I'll get into the garden."

Gingerly, she ate a little bit and held her hand on top of her head to see which way she was growing. She was quite surprised to find that she remained the same size. To be sure, this is what generally happens when one eats cake.

But Alice had gotten so used to unexpected things happening that it seemed quite dull and stupid for life to go on in the same old way.

So she set to work and ate every morsel of the cake.

CHAPTER TWO

The Pool of Tears

"Life is getting curiouser and curiouser," cried Alice, who was so surprised that for the moment she quite forgot how to speak good English. "Now I'm opening out like the largest telescope in the world."

Looking down at her feet, she saw to her amazement that they were so far away they were almost out of sight. "Good-bye, feet!" she called.

"Goodbye, Feet!"

"Oh, my poor little feet, I wonder who will put on your shoes and stockings for you now, dears? I'm sure I won't be able. I shall be much too far off to trouble myself about you.

"You must manage the best way you can—but I must be kind to them," thought Alice, "or perhaps they won't walk the way I want to. Let me see. I'll give them a new pair of boots every Christmas."

And she went on planning to herself how she would manage it. "How funny it'll seem, sending presents to one's own feet. Oh, what nonsense I'm talking."

Just at that moment her head hit the roof of the hall. In fact, she was now more than nine feet tall.

At once Alice picked up the little gold key and hurried off to the garden door. Poor Alice. It was all she could do, lying down on one side, to look through into the garden with one eye. To get through was more hopeless than ever.

Sad and frustrated, she burst into tears.

"You ought to be ashamed of yourself," Alice scolded herself, "a great big girl like you crying this way. Stop this moment, I tell you." But Alice went on crying all the same, shedding gallons of tears until there was a large pool around her about four inches deep, reaching half way down the hall.

After a while she heard the pitter-patter of feet in the distance. Hastily she dried her eyes, so she could see who was coming. It was the White Rabbit returning, splendidly dressed, with a pair of white kid gloves in one hand and a large fan in the other.

He came trotting along in a great hurry, muttering to himself. "Oh! The Duchess, the Duchess! Oh! Think how angry she'll be, if I've kept her waiting!"

Alice was so desperate that she was ready to ask anyone for help, so when the Rabbit came near, she approached him timidly. "If you

The Rabbit Dropped His Gloves and Fan.

please, Sir—"

To her surprise the Rabbit twitched and jerked violently, dropped his white kid gloves and fan and scurried away into the darkness as fast as he could go.

Alice picked up the fan and gloves and, as the hall was very hot, she fanned herself madly. All the while she continued talking.

"Dear, dear! How odd everything is today," she said in a bewildered tone of voice. "Yesterday things went on just as usual. I wonder if I've been changed in the night? Let me think. Was I the same person when I got up this morning? I almost think I can remember feeling a little different. But if I'm not the same, who in the world am I? Ah, that's the great puzzle!"

And then she began thinking of all the other girls she knew that were the same age as herself, to see if she could have been exchanged for any of them.

"I'm sure I'm not Ada," she said, "for her hair is in such long ringlets, and mine is not in ringlets at all. I'm sure I can't be Mabel, for I know all sorts of things, and she knows such a very little. Besides, she's she, and I'm I, and— oh, dear, how puzzling it all is!"

As Alice spoke, the wheels in her mind kept turning. "I'll try to remember if I still know all the things I used to know. Let me see: four times seven is—oh, dear! I shall never get to twenty at that rate. Let's try geography. London is the capital of Paris, and Paris is the capital of Rome— no, that's all wrong, I'm certain. I must have been changed for Mabel. I'll try and say 'How doth the little'—"

With that she crossed her hands in her lap, as if she was repeating lessons. But her voice sounded hoarse and strange, and the words did not come out quite the same way they used to:

"How doth the little crocodile

"Four Times Seven Is—"

Improve his shining tail,
And pour the waters of the Nile
On every golden scale!

"How cheerfully he seems to grin
How neatly spreads his claws,
And welcomes little fishes in,
With gently smiling jaws!"

"I'm sure those are not the right words," said Alice, and her eyes filled with tears again, as she went on, "I must be Mabel after all. I shall have to go and live in that funny little house and have hardly any toys at all to play with and ever so many lessons to learn. No, I've made up my mind about it. If I'm Mabel, I'll stay down here. It'll be no use for anyone to put their head down the hole and say, 'Come up again, dear!' I shall only look up and ask, 'Who am I, then?'"

Alice took a deep breath, paused for a

minute and then continued. "Tell me who I am first. If I like that person, I'll come up. If not, I'll stay down here till I'm somebody else—but, oh dear!" the bewildered girl cried with a sudden burst of tears, "I do wish someone would put their head down here. I am so very tired of being alone!"

As she spoke, Alice looked down at her hands and was surprised to see that she had put on one of the Rabbit's little white kid gloves while she was talking.

"How could I have done that?" she wondered. "I must be growing small again."

She got up and went to the table to measure herself by it and found that, as nearly as she could guess, she was now about two feet high and was continuing to shrink rapidly. She soon realized that the fan she was holding was the cause of this. She dropped it hastily just in time to save herself from shrinking away altogether.

Up to Her Chin in Salt Water

"That was a narrow escape," said Alice, frightened at the sudden change, but very glad to find herself still in existence, "and now for the garden."

The determined girl ran quickly back to the little door, but it was shut again, and the gold key was lying on the glass table as before. "Things are worse than ever," thought Alice, "for I never was as small as this before, never. And I declare it's too bad, that it is!"

At that moment her foot slipped and in another moment, splash! She was up to her chin in salt water. Alice first thought she had fallen into the sea, but then she realized that she was in the pool of tears. which she had made when she was nine feet tall.

"I wish I hadn't cried so much," said Alice as she swam about, trying to find her way out, "I shall be punished for it now by being drowned in my own tears. That will be odd, to be sure. However, everything is odd today."

Just then she heard something splashing about in the pool not far away. At first she thought it must be a walrus or a hippopotamus. But then she remembered how small she was now and realized the creature was a mouse.

"Would it be of any use now," thought Alice, "to speak to this mouse? Everything is so strange down here, that I should think it very likely he can talk. At any rate, there's no harm in trying."

So she began. "Oh, Mouse," she wailed, "do you know the way out of this pool? I am very tired of swimming about here. Oh, Mouse!"

Alice thought this must be the right way of speaking to a mouse, although she had never done such a thing before.

The Mouse looked at her rather inquisitively and seemed to wink with one eye. Yet he said nothing.

"Perhaps he doesn't understand English,"

"Oh, Mouse," She Wailed.

thought Alice. "I daresay he's a French mouse that came over with William the Conqueror," However, the imaginative girl, with all her knowledge of history, didn't have the slightest notion how long ago anything had happened.

So she asked him the first question that appeared in her French lesson book, "Ou est ma chatte?" She knew, of course, that in English that meant, "Where is my cat?"

Suddenly the Mouse leaped out of the water and quivered all over with fright.

"Oh, I beg your pardon," cried Alice hastily, afraid she had hurt the poor animal's feelings. "I quite forgot you don't like cats."

"Not like cats!" the Mouse shrieked. "Would you like cats if you were me?"

"Well, perhaps not," admitted Alice in a soothing tone, "but don't be angry about it. How I wish I could show you our cat, Dinah. I think you'd take a fancy to cats, if you would only meet her."

"She is such a dear, sweet thing," Alice went on, as she swam lazily about in the pool. "She sits purring so nicely by the fire, licking her paws and washing her face. She's good at catching mice, too. Oh, I beg your pardon!" cried Alice again, as she saw the Mouse bristle, "We won't talk about Dinah anymore, if you'd rather not."

"We, indeed," cried the Mouse, who was trembling down to the end of his tail. "As if I would talk about such a subject. Our family always hated cats—nasty, low, vulgar things! Don't let me hear the name again."

"I won't indeed," said Alice, anxious to change the subject. "Are you—are—you—fond —of—of—dogs?"

The Mouse did not answer, so Alice continued eagerly. "There is such a nice little dog near our house—a bright-eyed terrier who fetches things when you throw them. He'll sit and beg for his dinner and all sorts of things.

It Was High Time to Go.

Actually he belongs to a farmer who says he kills all his rats and—oh, dear," cried Alice, "I'm afraid I've offended you again."

How right she was, for the Mouse was swimming away as fast as he could go and making quite a commotion in the pool, too.

So Alice called softly after him, "Mouse, dear. Do come back, and we won't talk about cats or dogs either, if you don't like them."

When the Mouse heard this, he turned around and swam slowly back to Alice. His face was quite pale, and he said in a low trembling voice, "Let us get to the shore, and I'll tell you the story of my life. Then you will understand why I hate cats and dogs."

It was high time to go. The pool was getting quite crowded with all the birds and animals that had fallen into it. Alice could not quite believe her eyes. She looked around at the great pool of water that had once been her very own tears. It was unusual enough that she had been so big that she could have cried a pool now big enough for her to swim in, and the Mouse as well. But now there was barely room for the two of them! All sorts of creatures were swimming in Alice's tears. There was a Duck and a Dodo, a big, rather clumsy bird that didn't fly; also a brilliantly colored parrot known as a Lory; an Eaglet and several other curious creatures. Alice led the way, and the whole party swam to shore.

Alice Led the Way.

CHAPTER THREE

A Caucus Race and a Long Tale

The creatures that assembled on the bank—the birds with their bedraggled feathers, the animals with their fur clinging to them, all dripping wet, cross and uncomfortable—were an odd-looking party.

The first question, of course, was how to get dry again. They had a little chat about this, and after a few minutes, Alice felt very much at ease with them. It was as if she had known them all her life.

Unfortunately she got into quite an argument with the Lory, who became sulky and would only say, "I'm older than you and must know better."

Alice was not sure that he did know better. Since she did not know how old he was, and he refused to tell her, she thought it was best just to drop the subject.

At last the Mouse, who seemed to be a person of some authority among them, called out, "Sit down, all of you, and listen to me. I'll soon make you dry enough."

They all sat down at once in a large circle with the Mouse in the middle. Alice kept her eyes upon him the whole time, for she felt sure she would catch a bad cold, if she did not get dry very soon.

"Ahem," said the Mouse with an important air. "Are you all ready? This is the driest thing I know." With that he launched into a long dull

"I Am Still Soaking Wet."

story about English history that nearly put the group to sleep.

"Ugh," said the Dodo with a shiver.

"I beg your pardon," replied the Mouse, frowning, but trying to be polite. "Did you say something?"

"I'm sorry, but I am still soaking wet," the poor, bored Dodo explained. "I think the best way to get dry is to have a caucus race."

"What in the world is a caucus?" inquired Alice when no one else said anything.

"Oh, it's—it's—a—a—meeting," said the Dodo, strutting around, flapping his wings, and trying to look important, too. "Yes, that's right—a meeting of people in a party. You know, like a political party. Someone told me all about it once, but I can't seem to remember who."

"I see," said Alice, anxious to follow the conversation. "Well, there's quite a party of us here today, certainly enough to hold a caucus.

But what, may I ask, is a caucus race?"

"I think the best way to explain it is just to do it," said the Dodo. With a great flourish he broke off a branch from a lilac bush and used it to mark out a race course in a sort of circle. Once he had done that, the big bird placed everyone in his party along the course at various spots here and there.

No one ever called, "One, two, three, go!" but all the creatures began running and stopping whenever they felt like it. Therefore, it was not easy to know when the race was over.

However, when they had been running half an hour or so and were quite dry again, the Dodo suddenly called out, "The race is over!"

"But who has won?" all the birds and animals cried, crowding around him, exhausted and out of breath.

It was a question the Dodo could not answer without a great deal of thought, and he stood for a long time with one finger pressed on

All the Creatures Began Running.

his forehead, while everyone waited in silence. At last the Dodo said, "Everybody has won, and everyone should get a prize."

"But who is to present the prizes?" cried a chorus of voices.

"Why Alice, of course," said the Dodo, pointing at her with one finger. The whole party crowded around her calling out, "Prizes! Prizes!"

Alice had no idea what to do, and in despair she reached into her pocket and pulled out a handful of candy which she passed around as prizes. Fortunately there was exactly one piece for each of the runners.

"But Alice must have a prize herself," the Mouse declared.

"Of course," the Dodo replied gravely. "What else have you got in your pocket?" he asked.

"Only a thimble," said Alice sadly.

"Hand it over," said the Dodo.

Then they all crowded around her once more, while the Dodo solemnly presented the thimble, saying, "We beg your acceptance of this elegant thimble." When he had finished, they all clapped and cheered.

Alice thought the whole thing was quite absurd, but the little group all looked so serious that she did not dare to laugh. Since she could not think of anything to say, she simply bowed and took the thimble, looking as serious as she could.

The next matter of business was for the little group to eat their candy. For awhile everything was in a state of confusion, as the large birds complained that they could not taste their candy, and the little ones choked and had to be patted on the back. However, when it was over at last, they sat down in a circle again.

"You promised to tell me all about yourself," said Alice to the Mouse, "and why it is you hate cats and dogs," she added in a whisper, half-

"It Is a Long Tail."

afraid that he would be offended again.

"Mine is a long and a sad tale," said the Mouse, turning to Alice and sighing.

"It is a long tail. I can see that," she answered, looking down in wonder at the Mouse's tail. "But why do you call it sad?"

As the Mouse began to talk, Alice was still puzzled and so her idea of his tale went something like this:

Fury said to a mouse, that he met in the house,
"Let us go to law: I will prosecute you.
Come, I'll take no denial, we must have the trial;
For really this morning I've nothing to do."
Said the Mouse to the cur, "Such a trial, dear sir,
With no jury or judge, would be wasting our breath."
"I'll be the judge, I'll be the jury,"

Said the cunning Old Fury,

"I'll try the whole cause and condemn you to death."

"You are not listening to me," said the Mouse to Alice, frowning. "You offend me by thinking such nonsense."

"I didn't mean it," pleaded poor Alice, "but you're so easily offended."

The Mouse only growled in reply and walked away.

"Please come back and finish your story," Alice called after him. And all the others joined in a chorus, "Please do."

But the Mouse only shook his head impatiently and walked a little faster.

"What a pity he wouldn't stay," sighed the Lory, as soon as the Mouse was out of sight.

An old Crab took the opportunity to say to her daughter, "Now my dear, let this be a lesson to you never to lose your temper."

"Hold your tongue, Ma," said the young

The Mouse Growled and Walked Away.

Crab, a little snappishly. "You're old enough to try the patience of an oyster."

"I wish I had our Dinah here," said Alice, addressing no one in particular. "She'd soon bring the Mouse back."

"And who is Dinah?" asked the Lory.

"Dinah's our cat," Alice replied eagerly, and her whole face lit up as she spoke. "You can't imagine how good she is at catching mice. And, oh, I wish you could see her chase the birds. Why, she'd just as soon eat a little bird as look at it."

The speech caused quite a sensation among the assembled party. Some of the birds fluttered their wings nervously and hurried off at once.

"I really must be getting home," said one old Magpie, as she got her belongings together. "The night air is hard on my throat."

A canary called to her children in a trembling voice, "Come along, everyone. It's high time you were in bed."

Giving various excuses, all the creatures moved on and left Alice alone.

"Oh, I wish I hadn't mentioned Dinah," she said to herself sadly. "Nobody seems to like her down here, and I'm sure she's the best cat in the world. Oh, my dear Dinah, I wonder if I shall ever see you again."

Here poor Alice sat down on a tree stump and began to cry. In a little while, however, she heard the pitter-patter of footsteps in the distance. She looked up expectantly, hoping that the Mouse had changed his mind and was coming back to finish his story.

"Oh, My Fur and Whiskers!"

CHAPTER FOUR

The Rabbit Sends in a Little Bill

It was the White Rabbit, trotting slowly back again, looking anxiously about, as if he had lost something. "The Duchess! The Duchess!" he muttered, "Oh, my dear paws! Oh, my fur and whiskers! She's going to get me executed! Where could I have dropped those things?"

Alice guessed that he was looking for his fan and white kid gloves and good-naturedly joined in the hunt, but the Rabbit's belongings were nowhere to be seen. Everything seemed to have changed since her swim in the pool. The great hall, the glass table, and the little door had all vanished completely.

Very soon the Rabbit noticed Alice and called to her gruffly, "Why, Mary Ann, what are you doing here? Run home this minute and fetch me a pair of gloves and a fan. Quick now."

"He has mistaken me for his housekeeper," said the frightened girl, who dashed off in the direction the Rabbit had indicated. "How surprised he'll be when he finds out who I am. But I better take him his fan and gloves, if I can find them."

Alice had not anymore said this, before she stumbled upon a neat little house. On the door was a brass plate engraved "W. Rabbit."

Without knocking, she went inside and hurried upstairs to find the fan and gloves before she ran into the real Mary Ann, who she

She Stumbled Upon a Neat Little House.

feared might order her out of the house.

"How odd it seems," Alice remarked to herself, "to be running an errand for a rabbit. I suppose Dinah will be sending me on errands next."

By this time she had wandered into a tiny little room where she found the fan and gloves on a table. Just as she was getting ready to leave, she spotted a bottle near the looking-glass. Although there was no label marked "DRINK ME", Alice uncorked the bottle and took a sip.

"I know something interesting is sure to happen," she murmured to herself, "whenever I eat or drink anything. I do hope this will help me grow large again, for I'm tired of being such a tiny little thing."

Alice began to grow much sooner than she had expected. Before she had drunk half the bottle, her head pressed against the ceiling, and she had to stoop down to keep her neck from being squeezed.

Quickly she put down the bottle and said to herself, "That's quite enough. I hope I won't grow anymore. As it is, I can't get out the door. I wish I hadn't drunk quite so much."

It was too late to wish that! Alice went on growing until she had to kneel down on the floor. In another minute there was so little room that she had to lie down completely with one elbow against the door and the other curled around her head. Still she went on growing. As a last resort, she put one arm out the window and one foot up the chimney. Luckily the little magic bottle had its full effect, and she grew no larger.

"It was much pleasanter at home," Alice recalled. "I wasn't always growing larger and smaller and being ordered about by mice and rabbits. I almost wish I hadn't gone down that rabbit hole. Yet it's rather curious, you know, this sort of life. When I used to read fairy tales,

"No, You Won't," Vowed Alice.

I thought that kind of thing never happened. Now here I am in the middle of one!"

Suddenly Alice heard a voice outside and stopped to listen. "Mary Ann! Mary Ann!" someone cried urgently. "Fetch me my gloves this moment."

Then came the pitter-patter of feet on the stairs. Alice knew it was the Rabbit coming to look for her. She trembled till the house shook, quite forgetting that she was now about a thousand times as large as the Rabbit and had no reason to be afraid of him.

Presently the Rabbit arrived at the door and tried to open it, but Alice pressed her elbow against it, and he could not get in. At that point she heard him mutter, "Then I'll go around and get in a window."

"No, you won't," vowed Alice. When she heard the Rabbit just under the window, she reached out her hand and grabbed for him. Although she did not catch him, she heard a shriek, a fall, and a crash of broken glass. She suspected that the Rabbit had fallen into a cucumber frame.

She waited for some time without hearing anything more. Then at last she heard the rumbling of a wagon and the sound of a good many people all talking at the same time.

Occasionally she made out a sentence or two. "Where's the ladder?—Bill's got the other—Bill, bring it here.—Catch hold of that rope—Will the roof hold up?—Watch that loose slate!—Oh, it's coming down.—Who's going to go down the chimney?—Here, Bill, you've got to go down the chimney."

"Oh, so Bill's got to come down the chimney, has he?" said Alice to herself. "Why, I wouldn't want to be in his place for the world. This fireplace is narrow, to be sure, but I think I can kick a little."

Alice put her foot up the chimney as far as she could and waited till she could hear a little

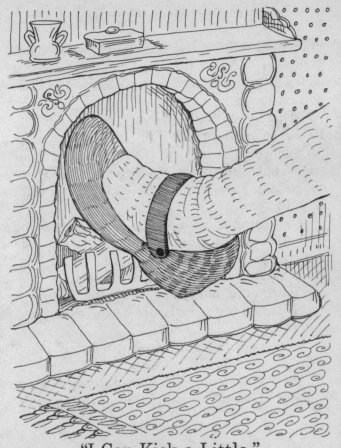

"I Can Kick a Little."

animal scratching and scrambling in the space above her. "That is Bill," she said and gave one sharp kick and waited to see what would happen next.

"There goes Bill!" everyone cried. Then the Rabbit shouted, "Catch him, you by the hedge!"

Silence followed, and then she heard other voices, babbling away. "Hold up his head. Don't choke him. How was it, old fellow? What happened to you?"

Last came a little, feeble, squeaking voice that Alice knew must be Bill. "All I know is something came at me like a Jack-in-the box, and I went flying up like a sky rocket."

"So you did, old fellow," cried the crowd.

"We must burn the house down," exclaimed the Rabbit.

"If you do, I'll send Dinah after you," Alice yelled as loud as she could.

There was dead silence instantly, and Alice thought to herself, "I wonder what they will do next? If they have any sense, they will take the roof off."

After a few minutes, Alice heard the Rabbit say, "A barrowful will do to begin with."

"A barrowful of what?" thought Alice.

To her surprise a shower of little pebbles came rattling against the window, and some hit her in the face. "I'll put a stop to this," she shouted. "You better not do that again."

This time all she heard was more silence.

To her amazement Alice noticed that the pebbles were all turning into little cakes. "If I eat one of those," she mused, "it's sure to make some change in my size. Since it can't possibly make me larger, it must make me smaller."

So she swallowed one of the cakes and was delighted to find that she began shrinking almost at once. As soon as she was small enough to get through the door, she ran out of the house and found a crowd of little animals and birds waiting outside.

An Enormous Puppy Was Looking at Her.

The poor little Lizard, Bill, was in the middle, being held up by two guinea pigs, who were giving him something out of a bottle.

They all made a dash at Alice the moment she appeared, but she ran off as fast as she could and soon found herself safe in a thick wood.

"The first thing I've got to do," Alice told herself, as she wandered about in the forest, "is to grow to my right size. The second thing is to find my way into that lovely garden. I think that will be the best plan."

It sounded like an excellent plan, no doubt. The only difficulty was that she didn't have the slightest idea of how to put it into motion. While she was peering about anxiously among the trees, she heard a sharp little bark just over her head. Immediately she looked up.

An enormous puppy was looking down at her with large round eyes and feebly stretching out one paw, trying to touch her.

"Poor little thing," said Alice, in a coaxing tone, and she tried hard to whistle to him. But she was terribly frightened at the thought that he might be hungry and might just eat her up in spite of all her coaxing.

Hardly knowing what she did, she picked up a stick and held it out at the puppy. He jumped off his feet way up into the air, and with a yelp of delight, he rushed at the stick.

Alice dodged behind a great thistle to keep from being run over by him. The moment she appeared on the other side, the puppy made another rush at the stick and tumbled head over heels in his hurry to get hold of it.

Alice, expecting any moment to be trampled under his feet, ran around the thistle again. Then the puppy began a series of short charges at the stick, running a little way forward each time and a long way back, barking loudly all the while. At last he sat down a good way off, panting, with his tongue hanging out

Off His Feet, Way Up in the Air

of his mouth. His large droopy eyes were half shut.

This seemed to Alice like a good opportunity to make her escape, so she set off at once. She ran till she was quite tired and out of breath and till the puppy's bark sounded faint in the distance.

"And yet what a dear little puppy it was!" said Alice, as she leaned against a buttercup to rest and fanned herself with one of the leaves.

"I should have enjoyed teaching him tricks very much, if only I'd been the right size to do it. Oh dear! I'd nearly forgotten that I've got to grow big again. Let me see—how am I going to do it? I suppose I should start by eating or drinking something, but the great question is, 'what?'"

Glancing around her at the flowers and blades of grass, she did not see anything that looked right under the circumstances. Finally she spotted a large mushroom just about her height, growing near her.

When she had looked under it and on both sides of it, it occurred to her that she might as well look and see what was on the top of it.

So Alice stood on tiptoe and peeped over the edge of the mushroom. Immediately her eyes met those of a large blue caterpillar sitting on top with his arms folded. This interesting creature was smoking a long hookah, better known as a water pipe, and not taking the slightest notion of her or of anything else.

"Who Are You?" He Asked.

CHAPTER FIVE

Advice from a Caterpillar

The Caterpillar and Alice looked at each other for some time in silence. At last the Caterpillar took the hookah out of his mouth and addressed her in a lazy, sleepy voice.

"Who are you?" he asked.

"I hardly know, Sir, just at present," Alice replied shyly. "I know who I was when I got up this morning, but I have changed several times since then."

"What do you mean by that?" said the Caterpillar sternly. "Explain yourself."

"I can't explain myself, I'm afraid, Sir," said Alice, "because I'm not myself, you see."

"I don't see," said the Caterpillar.

"I'm afraid I can't put it more clearly," Alice replied politely, "for I don't understand it myself. It's very confusing being so many different sizes in one day."

"No, it isn't," replied the Caterpillar.

"Well, perhaps you haven't found this out for yourself yet," Alice said. "But when you have to turn into a chrysalis, your next stage of life, and after that into a beautiful butterfly, I should think you will find it rather odd. Don't you think so?"

"Not a bit," said the Caterpillar.

"Well, perhaps your feelings are different from mine," Alice retorted. "All I know is that it would feel very odd to me."

"You!" cried the angry Caterpillar. "Who are

"It's Very Confusing," Alice Said.

you?" he asked again.

Now they were back at the beginning of their conversation. Alice was more than a little irritated at the Caterpillar for making such very sharp remarks. She stood up straight and tall, pulled in her breath, and said very seriously, "I think you ought to tell me who you are first."

"Why?" asked the Caterpillar.

"Another ridiculous question," thought Alice who was at a complete loss for an answer. Since the Caterpillar seemed to be in a very unpleasant mood, she stomped off.

"Come back!" he called. "I've something important to say to you."

This was a promising turn of events, so Alice wheeled around and came back. After all, he might tell her something worth hearing. For some minutes the Caterpillar puffed away without speaking, but at last he folded his arms, took the hookah out of his mouth, and said, "So you think you've changed, do you?"

"I'm afraid I have, Sir," said Alice.

"What size do you want to be?"

"Oh, I'm not particular as to size," Alice replied hastily. "I'm just tired of changing so often, you know.

"I don't know," said the Caterpillar.

Alice said nothing. She had never been contradicted so much in all her life, and she knew she was close to losing her temper.

"Are you content now?" asked the Caterpillar.

"Well, I should like to be a little larger, Sir, if you wouldn't mind," answered Alice. "Three inches is such a wretched height to be."

"It is a very good height indeed!" retorted the Caterpillar angrily, rearing himself upright as he spoke. You see, he was exactly three inches high himself.

"But I'm not used to it," pleaded Alice.

"You'll get used to it in time," said the

One Side of What? Alice Wondered.

Caterpillar. With that he put the hookah in his mouth and began smoking once more.

This time Alice waited patiently until the creature chose to speak again. In a minute or two the Caterpillar took the hookah out of his mouth, yawned once or twice, and shook himself.

Then he got down off the mushroom and crawled away into the grass, remarking as he went, "One side will make you grow taller, and the other side will make you grow shorter."

One side of what? The other side of what? Alice wondered.

"Of the mushroom," answered the Caterpillar, just as if she had asked the questions out loud. In another moment the Caterpillar had disappeared completely.

Alice remained looking thoughtfully at the mushroom for a minute. Then she stretched her arms around it as far as they would go and broke off a bit of the edge with each hand.

"And now which is which?" she asked herself, nibbling a little of the right hand bit to see the effect. The next moment her chin struck her foot in a sudden violent blow.

Her chin was pressed so closely against her foot that she was hardly able to open her mouth. However, she finally managed to swallow a morsel of the left hand bit.

"My head's free at last," said Alice in a tone of delight which changed to alarm the next minute when she found her shoulders were nowhere to be seen. All she could see, when she looked down, was an immense length of neck which seemed to rise like a stalk out of a sea of green leaves that lay far below her.

"What can all that green stuff be?" asked Alice. "Where have my shoulders gone to? Oh, my poor hands, how is it I can't see you?"

As there seemed to be no way of getting her hands up to her head, she tried to get her head down to them. She was delighted to find that

Her Shoulders Were Nowhere to Be Seen.

her neck would bend easily in any direction, like a serpent. She succeeded in curving it down into a graceful zigzag and was going to dive in among the leaves when she discovered they were the tops of the trees.

A loud hiss made her draw back in a hurry. A large pigeon had flown up into her face and was beating her with its wings.

"Serpent!" screamed the Pigeon.

"I'm not a serpent," said Alice indignantly. "Let me alone."

"Serpent, I say again," repeated the Pigeon. "Oh, how I detest them. I have been on the lookout for serpents night and day. Why, I haven't had a wink of sleep in weeks."

"I'm very sorry you've been annoyed," said Alice, who was beginning to sympathize with the distressed bird.

"Just as I'd taken the highest tree in the woods," continued the Pigeon, raising its voice to a shriek, "and was beginning to think I was free of them, one comes wriggling down from the sky."

"But I'm not a serpent, I tell you," said Alice. "I'm a—I'm a—"

"Well! What are you?" inquired the Pigeon.

"I'm a little girl," explained Alice, rather doubtfully, remembering the number of changes she had gone through that day.

"A likely story indeed," said the Pigeon with contempt. "I've seen a good many little girls in my time, but never one with such a neck as that. No, no. You're a serpent, and there's no use denying it. I suppose you'll be telling me next that you never tasted an egg."

"Certainly I have tasted eggs," said Alice, who was a very truthful girl. "Little girls eat eggs quite as often as serpents do, you know."

"I don't believe it," said the Pigeon, "but if they do, why, then they're a kind of serpent. That's all I can say."

This was such a new idea to Alice that she

"A Little Girl or a Serpent?"

was silent for a minute or two. The pause gave the Pigeon the opportunity to add, "You're looking for eggs. I know that well enough. What does it matter to me whether you're a little girl or a serpent?"

"It matters a good deal to me," said Alice hastily, "but as it happens, I'm not looking for eggs. If I was, I wouldn't want yours. I don't like them raw."

"Well, be off then," said the Pigeon in a sulky tone, as he settled down again in his nest.

Alice crouched down among the trees as well as she could, for her neck kept getting tangled among the branches. Every now and then she had to stop and untwist it.

After while she remembered that she still held the pieces of mushroom in her hands, so she began nibbling first at one and then at the other, growing sometimes taller and sometimes shorter. Finally she was able to bring herself down to her usual height.

It felt quite strange at first to be her normal size, but she got used to it in a few minutes. Soon she was talking to herself as usual. "There's half my plan done now. The next thing is to get into that beautiful garden, but how am I going to do that, I wonder?"

Just as she spoke, she came upon an open space with a little house on it about four feet high. "Whoever lives here," thought Alice, "would be frightened out of their wits if they met me right now while I was this height."

Without wasting a minute, she began nibbling at the right-hand bit of mushroom again and did not venture near the house till she had shrunk to only nine inches in height.

A Little House About Four Feet High

CHAPTER SIX

Pig and Pepper

For a minute or two Alice stood looking at the house and wondering what to do next, when suddenly an elegantly dressed footman came running out of the wood. The astonished girl thought he was a footman because of his uniform. Otherwise, judging by his face, she would have said he was a fish.

The Fish-Footman rapped loudly on the door, which was opened by another footman, equally well outfitted, with a round face and large eyes like a frog. Alice noticed that both footmen had powdered hair that curled all over their heads. Growing more curious by the minute, she crept out of the wood to listen to their conversation.

From under his arm the Fish-Footman produced an enormous letter, nearly as large as himself, which he handed over to the other, saying solemnly, "For the Duchess. An invitation from the Queen to play croquet."

The Frog-Footman repeated, in the same solemn tone, just changing the word order, "From the Queen. An invitation for the Duchess to play croquet."

Then they both faced each other and bowed low. As they did so, their curls got all tangled up together.

Alice laughed so loudly at this hilarious sight that she had to run back into the wood, so they would not hear her. When she peeped

The Other Was Sitting on the Ground.

out, the Fish-Footman was gone, and the other gentleman was sitting on the ground near the door.

Alice walked timidly up to the door and knocked.

"There's no use in knocking," said the Frog-Footman, "for two reasons. First, because I'm on the same side of the door as you. Secondly, because they're making so much noise inside, no one could possibly hear you."

Without a doubt, there was an extraordinary amount of noise within—a constant howling and sneezing. Every now and then Alice heard a tremendous crash, as if a dish or kettle had been broken to pieces.

"Please, please," said Alice, "how am I to get in?"

"There might be some sense in your knocking," said the Frog-Footman, "if we had the door between us. For instance, if you were inside, you might knock, and I could let you out."

"But how am I to get in?" Alice repeated.

"I shall sit here," the Frog-Footman remarked, not answering her question, "till tomorrow."

At that moment the door of the house opened. A large plate came flying out, headed straight at the Frog-Footman's head. Fortunately it just grazed his nose and broke into pieces against one of the trees behind him.

"Or the next day, maybe," the Footman continued, as if nothing had happened.

"Oh, there's no use talking to him," Alice said, throwing up her hands in disgust. "He's a perfect idiot."

With that, she opened the door and went inside the house. She found herself standing in a large kitchen, which was full of smoke. There sitting on a three-legged stool sat the Duchess, cuddling a baby. The cook was leaning over the fire, stirring a large cauldron of soup.

The Duchess Cuddling a Baby

"There is certainly too much pepper in that soup," Alice declared, sneezing loudly.

There was certainly too much pepper in the air. Even the Duchess sneezed occasionally. As for the baby, the poor thing was sneezing one minute and howling the next.

The only two creatures in the kitchen who weren't sneezing were the cook and a large cat, which was lying on the hearth and grinning from ear to ear.

"Would you please tell me," Alice asked the Duchess timidly, "why that cat grins like that?"

"He's a Cheshire Cat," answered the Duchess impatiently, "and that's why. Pig!"

Suddenly Alice began to shake all over, quite alarmed by the Duchess's shrill tone of voice. Then, as the frightened girl realized that the last remark was addressed to the baby, she gathered up her courage and continued, "I didn't know Cheshire Cats always grinned. In fact I didn't know that cats *could* grin."

"They all can," replied the Duchess bluntly, glaring at Alice, "and most of them do."

"I don't know of any that do," Alice said politely.

"You don't know much," retorted the Duchess, "and that's a fact."

Alice didn't like that remark and decided it would be best to change the subject. The cook chose that moment to take the soup cauldron off the fire and began to throw everything in sight at the Duchess and the baby.

"Please, watch what you're doing," cried Alice, jumping up and down in a fit of terror. "You don't want to hit the baby!" With that, a large sauce pan flew by, narrowly missing the child.

"If everybody minded their own business," the Duchess growled, "the world would go around a great deal faster than it does."

"Which would not be an advantage," replied Alice, anxious to show off her knowledge. "You

"You Can Play with the Baby."

see, the world only takes twenty-four hours to turn around on its axis. You wouldn't want night and day to go any faster."

"Speaking of axes," cried the Duchess at the top of her lungs. "Chop off her head!"

Alice glanced rather anxiously at the cook to see if she took the hint, but she was busy stirring the soup and did not appear to be listening.

All this time the Duchess, who seemed very agitated, sat holding the baby, singing a lullaby, but shaking the child at the end of each verse. The poor infant cried so loudly that Alice could hardly hear the words.

"Here! You can play with the baby, if you like," the Duchess said, flinging the child at Alice. "I have to go play croquet with the Queen."

Now Alice was very anxious to take good care of her young charge and rocked it tenderly in her arms. However, she couldn't help but notice that this baby was a rather strange one, with a turned-up nose, more like a snout than a nose. Not only that, but its eyes were extremely small for that of a baby.

When the infant first began to grunt, Alice thought it must be sobbing. So she looked into its eyes to see if there were any tears. But there weren't any. "If you're going to turn into a pig," said Alice quite seriously, "I'll have nothing more to do with you."

The next time the creature grunted so loudly that Alice was alarmed. There was no mistake about it now. The baby had definitely turned into a pig. So Alice set it down and was quite relieved to see it trot quietly into the wood.

"If it had grown up," Alice said to herself, "it would have made a dreadfully ugly child, but it makes a pretty handsome pig, I think."

As she walked away, Alice was startled to see the Cheshire Cat, sitting on the bough of a

The Baby Had Definitely Turned into a Pig.

tree a few yards away.

The Cat grinned broadly when he saw Alice. He looked quite good-natured, she thought. Still he had very long claws and a great many teeth, so Alice thought he should be treated with respect.

"Cheshire-Puss," she began, rather timidly, for she didn't know whether he would like the name.

However, the Cat only grinned a little more. He's pleased so far, thought Alice, and she went on, "Would you tell me, please, which way I ought to go from here?"

"That depends a great deal on where you want to go," said the Cat.

"I don't much care where—" said Alice.

"Then it doesn't matter which way you go," interrupted the Cat.

"So long as I get somewhere," Alice explained.

"Oh, you're sure to do that," remarked the

Cat, "if you only walk long enough."

"Tell me," Alice asked, "what sort of people live around here?"

"In that direction," said the Cat, waving his right paw, "lives a Hatter and in that direction," he said, waving the other paw, "lives the March Hare. Visit either one you like. They're both mad."

"But I don't want to live among mad people," Alice remarked.

"Oh, you can't help that," said the Cat. "We are all mad here. I'm mad. You're mad."

"How do you know I'm mad?" asked Alice.

"You must be," said the Cat, "or you wouldn't have come here."

Alice didn't think that proved anything at all. However, she continued, "How do you know that you're mad?"

"To begin with," said the Cat, "a dog's not mad. Do you agree?"

"I suppose so," said Alice.

He Vanished Right Before Her Eyes.

"Well, then," the Cat continued, "a dog growls when it's angry and wags its tail when it's pleased. Now I growl when I'm pleased, and my tail wags when I'm angry. Therefore, I'm mad."

"I call it purring, not growling," said Alice.

"Call it what you like," said the Cat. "Are you going to play croquet with the Queen today?"

"I should like to very much," said Alice, "but I haven't been invited yet."

"Look for me there," said the Cat smiling, and vanished right before her eyes.

CHAPTER SEVEN

A Mad Tea Party

Alice was not terribly surprised when the Cat disappeared because she was getting used to strange things happening. While she was still staring at the spot where he had been sitting, her new furry friend suddenly appeared again.

"By the way, what became of the baby?" he wanted to know.

"It turned into a pig," Alice answered very

"What Became of the Baby?"

quietly, just as if the Cat's return had been perfectly natural.

"I thought it would," said the Cat and vanished again.

Alice waited a little while, half expecting to
see him again. When he did not appear, she
walked away in the direction of the March
Hare's house.

"Perhaps since this is May, he won't be rav-
ing mad," Alice said to herself, "at least not so
mad as he was in March." As she spoke, she
looked up, and there was the Cat again,
perched on a tree branch.

"Did you say 'pig' or 'fig'?" asked the Cat.

"I said 'pig'," replied Alice, "and I wish you
wouldn't keep appearing and disappearing so
suddenly. Goodness, you make me dizzy."

"All right," said the Cat. This time he vanished slowly, beginning with the end of his tail
and ending with the grin, which remained
some time after his body had departed.

"Well, I've often seen a cat without a grin," thought Alice, "but a grin without a cat? It's the most curious thing I've ever seen in my life."

The March Hare's house was not far down the road. Alice thought it must be his house because the chimneys were shaped like ears and the roof was thatched with fur. It was such a large house, that she did not go near it until she had nibbled some more of the left-hand bit of mushroom and grown to a height of two feet.

A table was set out under a tree in the front yard, and the March Hare and the Hatter were having tea there. Between them sat a Dormouse who was fast asleep. His companions were using him as a cushion, resting their elbows on him and talking away over his head.

Very uncomfortable for the Dormouse, thought Alice, but since he's asleep, I suppose he doesn't mind.

The table was a large one, but the three

"No Room! No Room!" They Cried.

friends were all crowded together at one corner. "No room! No room!" they cried, when they saw Alice coming.

"There's plenty of room," said Alice indignantly, and she sat down in a large arm chair at the end.

"Have some wine," the March Hare said politely.

Alice looked all around the table, but there was nothing on it but tea. "I don't see any wine," she remarked.

"There isn't any," said the March Hare.

"Then it wasn't very nice of you to offer it," Alice said, more than a little annoyed.

"It wasn't very nice of you to sit down without being invited," replied the March Hare.

"I didn't know it was your table," answered Alice. "It's set for a lot more people than three."

The Hatter opened his eyes very wide, but all he said was, "Why is a raven like a writing desk?"

"I believe I can guess the answer to that," she said.

"Do you mean that you think you can find out the answer to it?" said the March Hare.

"Exactly," said Alice.

"Then you should say what you mean," the March Hare went on.

"I do," Alice hastily replied, "at least I mean what I say. That's the same thing, you know."

"Not the same thing at all," cried the Hatter. "Why, you might just as well say that 'I see what I eat' is the same thing as 'I eat what I see'."

"You might just as well say," added the Dormouse, who seemed to be talking in his sleep, "that 'I breathe when I sleep' is the same thing as 'I sleep when I breathe'."

"It is the same thing for you," chuckled the Hatter. He and the March Hare laughed hysterically.

Here the conversation stopped, and the

"You Should Say What You Mean."

party sat silent for a minute, while Alice tried to remember everything she knew about ravens and writing desks, which wasn't much.

The Hatter was the first to break the silence. "What day of the month is it?" he asked Alice. He had taken his watch out of his pocket and was looking at it uneasily. Every now and then he shook it and held it to his ear.

"The fourth," Alice said.

"You're off by two days," sighed the Hatter. "I told you butter would damage the works of my watch," he added, staring angrily at the March Hare.

"But it was the best butter," the March Hare replied meekly.

"Yes, but some crumbs must have gotten in as well," the Hatter grumbled.

With that the March Hare took the watch and dipped it into his tea. "It was the best butter, you know."

"What a funny watch," Alice remarked,

looking over his shoulders. "It tells the day of the month, but it doesn't tell what time it is."

"Why should it?" muttered the Hatter. "Does your watch tell you what year it is?"

"Of course not," Alice replied at once, "but that's because it stays the same year for such a long time."

"Which is just the case with mine," said the Hatter.

Alice was terribly puzzled. The Hatter's remark didn't have any real meaning. Yet it was certainly English.

"I don't quite understand you," she said, as politely as she could.

"The Dormouse is asleep again," said the Hatter, and he poured some hot tea on the poor little fellow's nose.

The Dormouse shook his head impatiently. Without opening his eyes, he said, "Of course. That's just what I was going to say myself."

"Have you guessed the riddle yet?" asked

"I Haven't the Slightest Idea."

the Hatter, turning to Alice again.

"No, I give up," Alice replied. "What's the answer?"

"I haven't the slightest idea," said the Hatter with a smirk.

"Nor I," said the March Hare.

Alice sighed wearily. "I think you might do something better with your time," she said, "than waste it asking riddles that have no answers."

"If you knew Time as well as I do," said the Hatter, "you wouldn't talk about wasting *it*. It's him, you know."

"No, I don't know what you mean," said Alice.

"Of course you don't," the Hatter said scornfully. "I dare say you never even spoke to Time."

"Perhaps not," Alice replied cautiously, "but I know I have to beat time when I learn music."

"Ah! That accounts for it," said the Hatter.

"Time won't stand a beating. Now, if you only kept on good terms with him, he'd do almost anything you liked with the clock. Suppose it was nine o'clock in the morning, just the time to open your books in school and get to work. You'd only have to whisper a word to Time, and he'd make the clock move in a twinkling. Soon it would be half-past one, time for lunch."

"That would be wonderful," said Alice thoughtfully, "but then I wouldn't be hungry."

"Not at first, perhaps," said the Hatter, "but you could keep the time at half-past one as long as you like."

"Is that the way you manage?" Alice asked.

The Hatter shook his head sadly. "Not I," he replied, "we quarreled last March just before he went mad," pointing with his teaspoon at the March Hare. "It was at a concert given by the Queen of Hearts and I had to sing:

'Twinkle, twinkle, little bat!
How I wonder what you're at!'

"That Would Be Wonderful," Said Alice.

Do you know the song, by any chance?"

"I've heard one like it," said Alice.

"It goes on, you know," the Hatter continued, "like this:

'Up above the world you fly
Like a tea-tray in the sky.
Twinkle, twinkle.'"

At this point the Dormouse shook himself
all over and began singing in his sleep, "Twinkle, twinkle, twinkle, twinkle —" He sang for
such a long time that they had to pinch him to
make him stop.

"I'd hardly finished the first verse," said the
Hatter, "when the Queen yelled, 'He's murder-
ing the time. Off with his head!' Ever since
then he won't do a thing I ask. It's always six
o'clock now."

During this entire conversation about time,
Alice had been doing some thinking on her
own. A bright idea came into her head. "Be
quiet, everyone," she said, tapping her spoon

against the china tea pot in front of her.

The others looked at her in great surprise.

Truth to tell, Alice was rather surprised at herself. To come up with a new idea was always a great achievement, she had been taught. But to come up with any idea at all, in the midst of such strange and strange-thinking creatures, seemed to her to be as extraordinary as all the things that had been happening ever since she had gotten here!

"We Never Have Time to Wash."

CHAPTER EIGHT

A Departure and An Arrival

Alice looked directly at them.

"Is the reason so many tea things are always out on the table because it's always six o'clock here?" She asked her three companions.

"Yes, that's it," said the Hatter with a sigh. "It's always tea time, and we simply never have the time to wash all the cups and saucers."

"Then you keep moving around the table to a fresh new place, is that it?" asked Alice.

"Exactly," said the Hatter. "We move each time things get used up."

"But what happens when you end up back at your starting place?"

"Let's change the subject," the March Hare interrupted, yawning. "I'm getting tired of talking about tea time. I vote the young lady tells us a story."

Alarmed by the March Hare's remark, Alice decided it was better not to mention her bright idea for the tea table. Instead she changed the subject and said simply, "I'm afraid I don't know a good story."

"Then the Dormouse shall tell a story," cried the Hare and the Hatter. "Wake up, Dormouse!" And they pinched him on both sides at once.

The Dormouse slowly opened his eyes. "I wasn't asleep," he said in a hoarse, feeble voice. "I heard every word you fellows were saying."

"Tell us a story," said the March Hare.

They Pinched Him on Both Sides at Once.

"And be quick about it," added the Hatter, "or you'll be asleep again before it's over."

"Once upon a time there were three sisters," the Dormouse began quickly. "Their names were Elsie, Lacie, and Tillie, and they lived at the bottom of a well."

"What did they live on?" asked Alice, who was always interested in what people had to eat and drink.

"They lived on treacle," said the Dormouse, after thinking it over for a minute or two.

"They couldn't have done that," Alice remarked. "Treacle is a medicine used to relieve the symptoms of poison. If they had eaten treacle, they'd have been ill."

"So they were," said the Dormouse, "very ill."

"But why did they live at the bottom of a well?" Alice wanted to know.

The Dormouse again took a minute or two to think about it and then he told her, "It was a treacle well."

"There's no such thing," Alice cried angrily.

"If you can't be polite, you can finish the story yourself," the Dormouse remarked, sulking.

"No, please go on," Alice said humbly. "I won't interrupt you again. I dare say there may be one."

"One indeed," said the Dormouse indignantly. However, he decided to go on. "And so these three sisters were learning to draw, you know."

"What did they draw?" asked Alice, quite forgetting her promise.

"Treacle," said the Dormouse.

"I want a clean cup," interrupted the Hatter. "Let's all scoot over one place."

The Hatter moved as he spoke, and the Dormouse followed him. The March Hare slipped into the Dormouse's place, and Alice took the seat of the March Hare. The Hatter

Alice Was Worse Off than Before.

was the only one who actually benefited from the move. Alice was worse off than before, as the March Hare had just upset the milk jug in his plate.

Alice did not wish to offend the Dormouse again, so she spoke very cautiously. "I don't understand. Where did the three sisters draw the treacle from?"

"You can draw water out of a water well," said the Hatter, "so I should think you could draw treacle out of a treacle well—eh, stupid?"

"But they were in the well," Alice said to the Dormouse.

"Of course they were," said the Dormouse, "well in. They were learning to draw all manner of things—everything that begins with an M—such as mouse-traps, the moon, memory, and muchness. You know you say that things are 'much of a muchness'. Did you ever see such a thing as a drawing of a muchness?"

"Really, now that you ask me," said Alice,

very confused, "I don't think—"

"Then you shouldn't talk," said the Hatter.

This rude behavior was more than Alice could bear, so she got up in disgust and walked off. Once or twice she looked back, hoping the Hatter and the Hare would call after her. However, the last time she saw them, they were trying to stuff the Dormouse into the teapot.

"I'll never go there again," Alice said, as she made her way through the wood. "That was the stupidest tea party I've ever been to in my whole life."

Just as she said this, she noticed that one of the trees had a door on the front of it. "That's very curious," she said, "but everything's curious today. I think I may as well go inside."

Once again Alice found herself in the long hall and near the little glass table. "Now, I'll manage better this time," she said to herself.

She began by taking the golden key and unlocking the door that led into the garden.

Stuffing the Dormouse into the Teapot

Then she nibbled at the mushroom she kept in her pocket till she was about a foot high.

Finally she walked down the little passage, and to her amazement and delight, arrived at last in the beautiful garden, among the bright flower beds and cool fountains.

A large rose tree stood near the garden entrance. The roses on it were white, but three gardeners were busy painting the petals red.

Alice thought this was very curious and went nearer to watch them work. Just as she walked up, she heard one of them say, "Look out now, Five. Don't go splashing paint over me like that."

"I couldn't help it," said Five, "Seven bumped my elbow."

At that Seven looked up and said, "That's right, Five. Always blame the other fellow."

"You better be careful what you say," said Five. "I heard the Queen remark only yesterday that you deserved to be beheaded."

"What for?" asked the one who had spoken first.

"That's none of your business, Two," said Seven.

"Yes, it is his business," said Five, "and I'll tell him. It was for bringing the cook tulip bulbs instead of onions."

Seven threw down his brush and said, "Well, of all the unjust things!" Suddenly he spotted Alice, as she stood watching them. With a flourish he and the other gardeners bowed low.

"Would you please tell me," asked Alice, "why you are painting those roses?"

Five and Seven said nothing but looked at Two, who said in a low voice, "Why, the fact is, Miss, the order was for a red rose tree, but we put a white one in by mistake. If the Queen finds out, we will all have our heads cut off. So you see we're doing our best before she comes to—"

Throwing Themselves on Their Faces

At that moment Five, who had been anxiously scouting the garden, called out, "The Queen! The Queen!"

Instantly the three gardeners threw themselves flat upon their faces. Footsteps resounded in the distance, and Alice looked around eagerly to see the Queen.

First, ten soldiers marched in carrying clubs. They were all shaped like the gardeners, oblong and flat, with their hands and feet located at their corners.

Next came ten courtiers, attendants in the royal court, who were decorated with diamond figures. They walked in two by two just as the soldiers had. Holding hands and dancing merrily along after the courtiers were the ten royal children—all covered with hearts.

Then came the guests, mostly Kings and Queens, who looked very splendid indeed. Running along in their midst was the White Rabbit, talking nervously, but smiling at nearly everything that was said. To Alice's surprise, he went flying by without even noticing her.

The Knave of Hearts, carrying the King's crown on a crimson velvet cushion, marched along proudly behind the Rabbit. Last of all in this grand procession, strolled the King and Queen of Hearts.

Alice was not sure whether she should fall down on her face like the three gardeners or not. The truth was she simply could not remember ever having heard of such a rule. "Besides," she thought, "what would be the purpose of a procession if people didn't get to see it?" So she stood still where she was and waited.

When the royal party arrived opposite Alice, they all stopped and looked at her intently. Beneath her dress, Alice felt her heart began to flutter rapidly, and her legs start to tremble ever so slightly. Her breath came

The Knave of Hearts Marched Along.

quickly in short bursts, and she felt dizzy and for a moment, she was afraid she might even faint.

Suddenly the Queen turned to the Knave of Hearts, and pointing at Alice, cried in a loud voice, "Who, pray tell, is she?"

Suddenly, all eyes were on Alice. She had never been so frightened in her life. She almost forgot that the Queen of Hearts had asked her name, and stood impatiently waiting for Alice's answer!

CHAPTER NINE

The Queen's Croquet Ground

"My name is Alice, so please your Majesty," answered the nervous girl, summoning up all her courage and bowing politely. Then she said to herself, "Why, they're only a pack of cards after all. I needn't be afraid of them."

"And who are these people?" asked the Queen, pointing to the gardeners, who were lying face-down around the rose tree. Since the pattern on their backs was the same as the

"Off with Her Head!"

rest of the pack, she could not tell whether they were gardeners, or soldiers, or courtiers, or three of her own children.

"How should I know?" asked Alice, surprised at her newfound courage. "It's no business of mine."

The Queen turned crimson with rage and screamed, "Off with her head!"

"Nonsense!" cried Alice loudly, and the Queen became silent.

"Remember, my dear," the King whispered to his wife, touching her gently on the arm, "she is just a young girl."

Angrily the Queen turned away from the King and addressed the three gardeners, who were still lying flat on their faces. "Get up!" she cried in a loud, shrill voice.

Two, Five, and Seven immediately jumped to their feet and began bowing to the King, the Queen, and all the royal children.

"What have you been doing here?" asked

the Queen, as she examined the rose tree carefully.

"May it please your Majesty," said Two humbly, falling down on one knee as he spoke. "We were trying—"

"I see," answered the Queen, most annoyed to discover that the roses had been painted. "Off with their heads!"

With that, the procession moved on, leaving three soldiers behind to behead the unfortunate gardeners, who rushed to Alice's side for protection.

"Don't worry. You won't be executed," promised Alice, and she quickly hid them in a large flowerpot that stood nearby.

The three soldiers wandered about for a minute or two, looking in vain for the gardeners. Finally they marched off after the others.

"Are their heads off?" screeched the Queen.

"Their heads are gone, if it please your Majesty," the soldiers shouted in reply.

She Hid Them in a Large Flowerpot.

"Wonderful," cried the Queen. "Can you play croquet, my dear?"

"Yes," returned Alice, who was relieved to escape such an unpleasant situation.

"Come on then," roared the Queen, and Alice joined the royal procession.

"It's—it's a very fine day," said a soft voice at her side. Alice looked down and there was the White Rabbit, staring up at her.

"It certainly is," the delighted girl agreed. "Where is the Duchess?"

"She's under sentence of execution," whispered the Rabbit. As he spoke, he looked anxiously over his shoulder.

"What for?" asked Alice.

"For boxing the Queen's ears—" the Rabbit began. Alice gave a little scream of laughter. "Oh, hush," the Rabbit whispered, "The Queen will hear you."

"Take your places everyone," shouted the Queen, and soon the game was underway.

What a strange croquet court it was. The grounds were composed entirely of ridges and furrows, so that it was impossible to hit the ball straight in any direction.

Not only that, but the croquet balls were live hedgehogs, and the mallets were real flamingoes. The soldiers had to double themselves up and stand on their heads and feet to form the arches.

For Alice the biggest difficulty was getting any of them to stand still long enough, so that she could play the game.

To make matters worse, the players were all playing at once, without waiting for their turns, quarreling and fighting for the hedgehogs. All of this upset the Queen to no end, and she went stomping about bellowing, "Off with his head!" and "Off with her head!"

Alice began to feel very uneasy because she feared that any minute the Queen might turn on her. "What will become of me?" the poor girl

She Realized It Was a Grin.

worried. "They're awfully fond of beheading people around here. It's a wonder that any one is left alive."

Just as she looked around for a way to escape, Alice noticed a curious sight in the air. After watching closely for a minute or two, she realized it was a grin.

"It's the Cheshire Cat," she cried, clapping her hands in delight. "Now I shall have somebody to talk to."

"How are you getting along?" asked the Cat, as soon as there was mouth enough for him to speak.

Alice waited till his eyes appeared and then nodded. There's no use speaking to him yet, she thought, till his ears have arrived or at least one of them.

In another minute the whole head appeared, and Alice began an account of the croquet game. "I don't think they play fairly at all," she complained. "They quarrel constantly and don't seem to have any rules at all. You have no idea how confusing it is, for all the wickets, mallets, and balls to be alive. For instance, there's the arch I've got to go through next, walking around at the other end of the court."

"How do you like the Queen?" asked the Cat in a low voice.

"Not at all," replied Alice, "she's so extremely—" Just then she noticed that the Queen was right behind her, listening, so she continued, "likely to win, that it's hardly worth finishing the game."

The Queen smiled and walked merrily on by.

"Who are you talking to?" asked the King, approaching Alice and gazing at the Cat's head with great curiosity.

"He's a Cheshire Cat," said Alice. "Allow me to introduce him."

"I don't like the look of him at all," said the

The Queen Walked Merrily On.

King. "However, he may kiss my hand, if he likes."

"I'd rather not," the Cat remarked.

"Don't be impertinent," replied the King, "and don't look at me like that." He stood behind Alice as he spoke.

"A cat may look at a king," said Alice. "I've read that in some book, but I don't remember where."

"Well, I won't tolerate it," cried the King with great authority. "My dear," he called to the Queen, who was passing by at that moment, "I wish you would have this cat removed."

Now the Queen had only one way of settling all difficulties, great or small. "Off with his head!" she cried, without even looking around.

"I'll fetch the executioner myself," said the King eagerly, and he hurried off.

Alice thought she might as well go back

and see how the croquet game was going, but the play was more confused than ever. Exasperated, she tucked her flamingo, who was constantly trying to escape, under her arm. She was surprised to find that a large crowd had gathered around the Cheshire Cat. There was a dispute going on between the executioner, the King, and the Queen, who were all talking at once. All the rest remained silent and looked quite uncomfortable.

The moment Alice appeared, the three people involved rushed to her side to tell her their side of the argument, begging her to settle the issue. Unfortunately they all talked at once, and Alice found it hard to understand a word they were saying.

The executioner's argument was that you could not cut off a head unless it was attached to a body. He stated emphatically that he had never done such a thing before, and he wasn't going to begin at this time of life.

The Executioner Shot Off Like an Arrow.

The King's argument was that anything that had a head could be beheaded. The Queen insisted that if something wasn't done soon, she'd have everyone executed, all around. This last remark was what made the whole party look so grave and anxious.

Alice could think of nothing else to say but, "The Cat belongs to the Duchess. You'd better ask her about it."

"She's in prison," the Queen said to the executioner, "fetch her here." And the executioner shot off like an arrow.

The Cat's head began fading away the moment the executioner departed. By the time he had returned with the Duchess, the head was gone completely. The King and the executioner ran wildly up and down looking for it, while the rest of the party went back to play croquet.

CHAPTER TEN

A Word from the Duchess

"You can't imagine how glad I am to see you again, you dear old thing," said the Duchess, as she tucked her arm affectionately into Alice's, and they walked off together.

Alice was delighted to find her in such a good mood and wondered if it could have been the pepper that had made her so rude and angry when they had met in the kitchen.

"When I am a Duchess," she said to herself,

They Walked Off Together.

though not in a very hopeful tone, "I won't have any pepper in my kitchen at all. Maybe it's pepper that makes people hot-tempered," she went on, very pleased at having discovered a new rule, "and vinegar that makes them sour and sugar that makes them sweet."

"You're thinking about something, my dear," said the Duchess right in her ear, "and that makes you forget to talk. I can't tell you just now what the moral of that is, but I shall remember it in a minute."

"Perhaps it doesn't have one," Alice remarked.

"Tut, tut, young lady," said the Duchess. "Everything's got a moral, if only you can find it."

As she spoke, she inched herself closer and closer to Alice until she had squeezed up right smack against her.

Alice didn't like this, first of all, because the Duchess was very ugly, and secondly, because she was resting her chin right on Alice's shoulder. And, oh, what a terribly sharp chin it was, too. However, Alice did not like to be rude, so she accepted the situation for the time being.

"The game's going on rather well now," she said in an effort to keep up the conversation.

"So it is," agreed the Duchess, "and the moral of that is—'Oh, 'tis love, 'tis love, that makes the world go round.'"

"Somebody said," Alice whispered, "that it's done by everybody minding their own business."

"Ah, well. It means very much the same thing," said the Duchess, digging her sharp little chin into Alice's shoulder, "and the moral of that is—'Take care of the sense, and the sounds will take care of themselves.'"

How fond she is of finding morals in things, Alice thought, trying vainly to make sense of this last remark.

"I dare say you are wondering why I don't

"He Might Bite," Alice Warned.

put my arm around your waist," the Duchess said after a pause. "The reason is that I'm not sure whether your flamingo is friendly or not. Shall I pet him and find out?"

"He might bite," Alice warned cautiously, holding the poor, weary, squirming bird tightly against her. She was not anxious for the Duchess to undertake such a risky experiment.

"Very true," agreed the Duchess. "Flamingoes and mustard both bite. And the moral of that is, 'Birds of a feather flock together.'"

"Only mustard isn't a bird," Alice pointed out.

"Right as usual," said the Duchess. "What a good way you have of putting things."

"Mustard is a mineral, I think," Alice said.

"Of course, it is," piped up the Duchess, who seemed eager to agree to everything that Alice said. "There's a large mustard mine over here. And the moral of that is 'The more there is of mine, the less there is of yours.'"

"Oh, I know," exclaimed Alice, who had not paid attention to this last remark. "Mustard is a vegetable. It doesn't look like one, but it is."

"I quite agree with you," said the Duchess, "and the moral of that is, 'Be what you would seem to be' or to put it more simply, 'Never imagine yourself not to be otherwise than what it might appear to others that what you were or might have been was not otherwise than what you had been would have appeared to them to be otherwise.'"

"I think I should understand that better," Alice said very politely, "if that were written down, and I could read it. But I can't quite follow it as you say it."

"That's nothing to what I could say, if I chose," the Duchess replied, very proud of herself. Smugly she gave her headdress a little push to keep it in place.

"Pray don't trouble yourself to say anything longer than that," said Alice.

"I Quite Agree with You," said the Duchess

"Oh, don't talk about trouble," cried the Duchess. "I'll make you a present of everything I've said as of now."

A cheap sort of present, thought Alice. I'm glad people don't give birthday presents like that. But she was careful to keep her thoughts to herself.

"Thinking again?" asked the Duchess with another dig of her sharp little chin.

"I've a right to think," said Alice curtly, for she was beginning to feel a trifle worried.

"Just about as much right," said the Duchess, "as pigs have to fly, and the mor—"

But here to Alice's great surprise, the Duchess's voice died away, even in the middle of her favorite word, "moral". Alice could feel the arm that was linked to hers begin to tremble. She looked up and there stood the Queen in front of them, with her arms folded, frowning like a thunderstorm.

"A fine day, your Majesty," the Duchess

began in a low weak voice.

"Now I give you fair warning," shouted the Queen, stamping her foot on the ground as she spoke, "either you or your head must be off and in no time, too. Take your choice."

The Duchess took her choice and hurried right off.

"Let's go on with the game," the Queen said to Alice, who was much too frightened to say a word. Obediently she followed the Queen back to the croquet ground.

The other guests had taken advantage of the Queen's absence and were resting in the shade. However, the moment they saw her, they hurried back to their places. In her usual bad temper, the Queen remarked that a moment's delay could cost them their lives.

All the time they were playing, the Queen never stopped quarreling with the other players and shouting, "Off with his head!" or "Off with her head!"

"Have You Seen the Mock Turtle?"

Those people whom she sentenced were taken into custody by the soldiers, who had to leave their jobs as arches to do this. It wasn't long before there were no arches left at all, and all the players, except the King, the Queen, and Alice were in custody and under sentence of execution.

Then the Queen, quite out of breath from all the yelling and screaming, approached Alice and asked, "Have you seen the Mock Turtle yet?"

"No," cried Alice wide-eyed, "I don't even know what a Mock Turtle is."

"It's the thing Mock Turtle soup is made from," explained the Queen.

"I never saw one or heard of one," said Alice.

"Come on then," said the Queen, "I want you to meet him. He'll tell you the story of his life."

As they strolled off together, Alice heard

the King announce to the company in general that they were all pardoned.

"Now that's a good thing," she said to herself, drawing a deep breath and relaxing for the first time in a long while. She had been quite unhappy about the large number of executions the Queen had ordered.

After the Queen and Alice had walked on for a good ways, they stumbled upon a Gryphon, lying fast asleep in the sun.

Now the Gryphon was a monster, more unusual than most, with the head, wings, and claws of an eagle and the body and hind parts of a lion. It even had a tail. Many people believed it also had the combined qualities of the eagle and the lion—watchfulness and courage.

The Queen, of course, was not like most people.

"Up, you lazy thing," she said to the monster sternly, "and take this young lady to meet

Now the Gryphon Was a Monster.

the Mock Turtle, so she can hear his story. I must go back and see what has happened to some of the executions I have ordered."

With that she walked off and left Alice alone with the Gryphon.

CHAPTER ELEVEN

The Mock Turtle's Story

Alice did not quite like the look of the Gryphon, but she thought it would be just as safe to stay with it as to pursue the ill-tempered Queen. So she sat down on a rock, smoothed out her skirt, and waited.

The Gryphon got up from its nap and rubbed its eyes. Then it watched the Queen until she was out of sight. "What fun," it chuckled, half to itself, half to Alice.

They Saw the Mock Turtle in the Distance.

"What do you mean, fun?" asked Alice.

"It's all the Queen's imagination really," said the Gryphon. "They never executes nobody, you know. Come on." The Gryphon may have had watchfulness and courage, Alice thought, but he didn't have very much in the way of grammar. But something else troubled her even more.

"Everybody says, 'Come on' here," thought Alice, as she trailed along slowly after the creature. "I have never been ordered about so much in my life, never."

They had not gone far before they saw the Mock Turtle in the distance, sitting sad and lonely on a little rock ledge. As they came nearer, Alice could hear him sighing as if his heart would break.

Suddenly she was overwhelmed with sympathy for him. "Why is he so unhappy?" she asked the Gryphon.

And the Gryphon answered very nearly in

the same words as before, "It's all his imagination really. He hasn't got no sorrow, you know. Come on."

So Alice and the Gryphon went up to the Mock Turtle, who looked at them with large eyes full of tears, but said nothing.

"This here young lady," announced the Gryphon, "she wants to know the story of your life, she do."

"I'll tell it to her," replied the Mock Turtle in a deep, hollow tone. "Sit down, both of you, and don't say a word till I've finished."

So they sat down, and nobody spoke for several minutes. Alice thought to herself, "I don't see how he can ever finish, if he doesn't begin." But she waited patiently, holding her hands in her lap in a very lady-like fashion.

"Once," said the Mock Turtle at last, with a deep sigh, "I was a real turtle."

These words were followed by a silence, broken only by an occasional exclamation of

How Can He Finish If He Doesn't Begin?

"Hjckrrh" from the Gryphon and the constant sobbing of the Mock Turtle.

Alice was very close to getting up and saying, "Thank you, Sir, for your interesting story." However, she could not help thinking there must be more to come, so she sat still and said nothing.

"When we were little," the Mock Turtle continued at last, more calmly, though still sobbing a little now and then, "we went to school in the sea. The teacher was an old turtle. We used to call him Tortoise."

"Why did you call him Tortoise if he wasn't one?" Alice asked.

"We called him Tortoise because he taught us," the Mock Turtle snapped. "Really, you are very dull."

"You ought to be ashamed of yourself for asking such a simple question," added the Gryphon, flicking his tail back and forth angrily. Then they both fell silent and stared at poor Alice, who wished with all her heart that she could sink right into the earth.

At last the Gryphon said to the Mock Turtle, "Go on, old fellow. Don't be all day about it."

"Yes, we went to school in the sea, though you may not believe it," the Mock Turtle began.

"I never said I didn't," interrupted Alice.

"You did," insisted the Mock Turtle.

"Hold your tongue!" cried the Gryphon in a menacing voice before Alice could speak again.

"We had the best of educations," the Mock Turtle continued. "In fact, we went to school every day."

"I've been to a day school, too," Alice piped up. "You needn't be so proud as all that."

"Were there extras?" asked the Mock Turtle anxiously.

"Yes," said Alice, "we learned French and music."

"And washing?" inquired the Mock Turtle.

"Certainly not," said Alice indignantly.

"I Couldn't Afford to Learn It."

"Ah! Then yours wasn't a really good school," replied the Mock Turtle, greatly relieved. "Now, at ours, they had at the end of the bill, 'French, music, and washing—extra.'"

"You couldn't have needed or wanted washing much," said Alice, "not if you lived at the bottom of the sea."

"I couldn't afford to learn it," said the Mock Turtle with a sigh. "I only took the regular course."

"What was that?" inquired Alice, moving closer to the Mock Turtle in an effort to understand everything he said.

"Reeling and Writhing, of course, to begin with," the Mock Turtle replied, "and then the different branches of Arithmetic—Ambition, Distraction, Uglification, and Derision."

"I never heard of Uglification," murmured Alice, totally confused at this point. "What is it?"

The Gryphon leaned back on his haunches

and threw up both his paws in surprise. "Never heard of uglifying?" it exclaimed. "You know what it is to beautify, I suppose?"

"Yes," said Alice slowly, "it means to-make-anything-prettier."

"Well, then," the Gryphon went on, "if you don't know what it is to uglify, you are a simpleton."

The monster's hostile attitude certainly didn't encourage Alice to ask any more questions on that particular subject. So she turned quickly to the Mock Turtle and inquired, "What else did you learn?"

"Well, there was Mystery," the Mock Turtle replied, counting off the subjects on his flappers, "Mystery, ancient and modern, Seaography, then Drawling and Stretching and Fainting with Coils."

"What was that like?" asked Alice.

"Well, I can't show you myself," the Mock Turtle said. "I'm too stiff, and the Gryphon

"You Are a Simpleton."

never learned it."

"Hadn't the time," explained the Gryphon. "I went to the Classics teacher though. He was an old crab, he was."

"I never went to his class," the Mock Turtle sighed regretfully. "He taught Laughing and Grief, they used to say."

"So he did. So he did," said the monster, taking his turn at sighing. This time both he and the Mock Turtle hid their faces in their scaly paws.

"And how many hours a day did you spend in school?" Alice asked.

"Ten hours the first day," answered the Mock Turtle, "nine hours the next, and so on."

"What a curious plan," exclaimed Alice, who never ceased to be surprised at anything she learned in this conversation.

"That's the reason they're called lessons," the Gryphon explained, "because they lessen from day to day."

This was quite a new idea to Alice, and she thought it over for awhile before she made her next remark. "Then the eleventh day must have been a holiday?"

"Of course it was," said the Mock Turtle.

"And how did you manage on the twelfth?" Alice asked eagerly.

"That's enough about those lessons," the Gryphon interrupted in a very decided tone. "Tell her something about the games."

The Mock Turtle sighed deeply and smoothed his brow with the back of one of his flappers. He looked at Alice sadly and tried to speak. For a minute or two his voice choked with sobs.

"It's just as if he has a bone caught in his throat," said the Gryphon, who set to work shaking and punching his poor forlorn friend on the back.

At last the Mock Turtle recovered his voice, and with tears running down his cheeks, he

"You Were Never Introduced to a Lobster

continued, "You may not have lived much under the sea—"

"I haven't," said Alice.

"Perhaps you were never even introduced to a lobster."

"I once tasted one," Alice started to say but thought better of it and said, "No, never."

"So you have no idea what a delightful thing a lobster quadrille can be," the Mock Turtle went on. "Well, you just be patient because I'm going to tell you all about it."

CHAPTER TWELVE

The Lobster Quadrille

"Now that you mention it, I would like to know what a lobster quadrille is," Alice replied eagerly. "I know it's a dance, but what sort of a dance is it?"

"Why, it's a square dance," said the Gryphon, jumping out in front of her and motioning with its paws. "First you form a line along the sea shore—"

"Two lines!" cried the Mock Turtle, who did

"What Sort of a Dance?"

not want to be left out of the conversation. "Seals, turtles, salmon, and so on. Then, when you've cleaned all the jellyfish out of the way—"

"That generally takes some time," interrupted the Gryphon.

"You advance twice—"

"Each time with a lobster as a partner," the Gryphon explained.

"Of course," agreed the Mock Turtle, "advance twice, set to partners—"

"Change lobsters and retire in the same order," continued the Gryphon.

"Then, you know," the Mock Turtle went on, "you throw the—"

"The lobsters!" shouted the Gryphon with a bound in the air.

"As far out to sea as you can."

"Swim after them!" screamed the Gryphon.

"Turn a somersault in the sea!" cried the Mock Turtle, dancing wildly about.

"Change partners again!" yelled the monster at the top of his lungs.

"Back to land again, and that's all the first figure in the dance," said the Mock Turtle, suddenly lowering his voice.

The two creatures, who had been rushing wildly about all this time, sat down again very sadly and looked at Alice.

"It must be a very pretty dance," she said quietly.

"Would you like to see a little of it?" asked the Mock Turtle.

"Very much indeed," Alice replied tactfully.

"Come, let's try the first figure," said the Mock Turtle to the Gryphon. "We can do it without lobsters, you know. Who shall sing?"

"Oh, you sing," said the Gryphon. "I've forgotten the words."

So they began dancing solemnly round and round Alice, every now and then stepping on her toes when they passed too closely. They

They Waved Their Front Paws.

waved their front paws in the air to keep time, while the Mock Turtle sang this song slowly and sadly:

> "Will you walk a little faster?" said a
>   whiting to a snail,
> "There's a porpoise close behind us, and
>   he's treading on my tail.
> See how eagerly the lobsters and the
>   turtles all advance!
> They are waiting on the shingle—Will
>   you come and join the dance?
> Will you, won't you, will you, won't you,
>   will you join the dance?
> You can really have no notion how
>   delightful it will be
> When they take us up and throw us, with
>   the lobsters out to sea!"
> But the snail replied, "Too far, too far,"
>   and gave a look askance—
> Said he thanked the whiting kindly, but
>   he would not join the dance.

Would not, could not, would not, could
    not, would not join the dance.
"What matters it how far we go?" his
    scaly friend replied.
"There is another shore, you know, upon
    the other side.
The further off from England the nearer
    is to France—
Then turn not pale, beloved snail, but
    come and join the dance.
Will you, won't you, will you, won't you,
    won't you join the dance?"

"Thank you, it's a very interesting dance to
watch," said Alice, relieved it was over at last.
"I do like that curious song about the fish
called a whiting."

"Oh, as to the whiting," said the Mock Turtle, "you've seen them, of course?"

"Yes," said Alice, "I've seen them at dinn—"
and stopped in the middle of the sentence.

"Thank You," Said Alice, Relieved.

"I don't know where dinn may be," the Mock Turtle replied, "but if you've seen them so often, then you know what they're like."

"I believe so," Alice answered thoughtfully. "They have their tails in their mouths and crumbs all over them."

"You're wrong about the crumbs," said the Mock Turtle, putting his flapper over his mouth to hide a smile. "Crumbs would all wash off in the sea. But they do have their tails in their mouths, and the reason is—" The Mock Turtle yawned and shut his eyes. "Tell her the reason and all that," he said to the Gryphon.

"The reason is," said the Gryphon, "that they would go with the lobsters to the dance. So they got thrown out to sea. So they had to fall a long way. So they got their tails stuck in their mouths and couldn't get them out again. That's all."

"Thank you," said Alice politely, "it's very interesting; I never knew so much about a whiting before."

"I can tell you more than that, if you like," said the Gryphon. "Do you know why it's called a whiting?"

"I never thought about it," said Alice. "Why?"

"It does the boots and shoes," the monster replied solemnly.

Alice was thoroughly puzzled. "Does the boots and shoes?" she repeated questioningly.

"Why, what are your shoes done with?" asked the Gryphon. "I mean, what makes them so shiny?"

Alice looked down at her shoes and thought a minute. "They're done with blacking, I believe."

"Boots and shoes under the sea," the Gryphon went on in a deep voice, "are done with whiting."

"And what are they made of?" Alice asked.

"Soles and eels, of course," the Gryphon replied impatiently. "Any shrimp could have told you that."

"Any Shrimp Could Have Told You That."

"If I'd been the whiting," said Alice, whose mind was still on the song, "I'd have said to the porpoise, 'Keep back, please! We don't want you with us!'"

"They had to have him with them," the Mock Turtle said. "No wise fish would go anywhere without a porpoise."

"Wouldn't it?" said Alice, quite surprised.

"Of course not," said the Mock Turtle. "Why, if a fish came to me and told me he was going on a trip, I would ask, 'With what porpoise?'"

"Don't you mean purpose?" asked Alice.

"I mean what I say," the Mock Turtle replied, somewhat offended.

"Come, let's hear some of your adventures," the Gryphon asked, sitting down beside Alice.

"I could tell you my adventures beginning with this morning," said Alice cautiously, "but there's no use going back to yesterday because I was a different person then."

So Alice began her story at the time when she first saw the White Rabbit. In the beginning she was a little nervous, but when the two creatures sat close to her, one on each side, and listened intently, she gained courage and continued.

"It's a very curious story," said the Gryphon when she had finished. "Repeat it if you will."

"How these creatures order me about," thought Alice. However, she got up and started to repeat her story, but her head was so full of the Lobster Quadrille that she hardly knew what she was saying and her words came out in a very strange way:

> "Tis the voice of the Lobster: I heard him declare
> 'You have baked me too brown, I must sugar my hair.'
> As a duck with its eyelids, so he with his nose

The Two Creatures Listened Intently.

Trims his belt and his buttons, and turns
  out his toes.
When the sands are all dry, he is gay as
  a lark,
And will talk in contemptuous tones of
  the Shark:
But, when the tide rises and sharks are
  around
His voice has a timid and tremulous
  sound."

"That all sounds like uncommon nonsense,"
said the Mock Turtle with a very strange
expression on his face.

Alice said nothing. She had sat down in the
grass with her face in her hands, wondering if
anything would ever happen in a natural way
again.

"I think you'd better stop now," said the
Gryphon, and Alice was only too glad to do so.
"Shall we try another figure of the Lobster

Quadrille?" the Gryphon asked next, "or would you like the Mock Turtle to sing you a song?"

"Oh, a song please, if the Mock Turtle would be so kind," Alice replied enthusiastically.

"Hmm. There's no accounting for taste," said the Gryphon, somewhat offended. "Sing her 'Turtle Soup' will you, old fellow?"

Just at that moment, they heard a cry of "The trial's beginning!" in the distance.

"Come on," cried the Gryphon. With that he grabbed Alice by the hand and rushed off with her. Faintly somewhere behind them on the wave of the breeze, they could hear the first chorus of the Mock Turtle's sad, soulful song:

"Beautiful Soup, so rich and green,
　　Waiting in a hot tureen
　　Who for such dainties would not stoop?
　　Soup of the evening, beautiful, beautiful
　　　Soup!"

But already Alice's mind was on what

The Gryphon Raced Along.

might be coming next, rather than on the poor Turtle's wail. Things happened and changed so quickly in this place, one could barely pay any attention to what was happening before something else completely different came in its place.

And soon, poor Alice couldn't think at all. It was all she could do to keep up with the Gryphon as he raced along, pulling her with him.

CHAPTER THIRTEEN

Who Stole the Tarts?

"What trial are we going to?" Alice panted, as she ran alongside the Gryphon.

But the monster only answered, "Come on," and ran all the faster. It was all poor Alice could do to keep up with him.

The King and Queen of Hearts were seated on their thrones when Alice and the Gryphon came dashing into the courtroom, all out of breath. A great crowd had assembled about

The King and Queen Were on Their Thrones

the royal pair—all sorts of birds and beasts, as well as the whole pack of cards.

The Knave was standing before them, in chains, with a soldier on each side to guard him. Near the King was the White Rabbit, with a trumpet in one hand, and a scroll of parchment in the other.

In the middle of the court stood a table. A dish of tarts had been placed there and they looked delicious and tempting indeed.

"I wish they'd get the trial over with," Alice thought, suddenly feeling quite hungry, "and pass around the refreshments." But since there seemed to be no chance of this, she began looking about her to while away the time.

Alice had never been in a court of justice before, but she knew a lot about it from books she had read. "That's the judge," she said to herself, "because he's wearing that enormous wig."

The judge, by the way, was the King, who

wore his crown over his wig. Unfortunately the wig was not at all becoming, and the King looked most uncomfortable.

"And that's the jury box," thought Alice, "and those twelve creatures are the jurors, I suppose." Alice thought to say creatures, because some of them were animals and some were birds. All of them were busy writing on slates.

"What are they doing?" Alice whispered to the Gryphon. "They can't have anything to put down yet."

"They're putting down their names," the Gryphon whispered, "so they don't forget them before the trial begins."

"Stupid things," Alice said in a loud voice.

"Silence in the court!" cried the White Rabbit. Immediately, the King put on his spectacles and looked around to see who was talking.

Alice could see almost as if she were looking over their shoulders, that all the jurors

One Didn't Know How to Spell "Stupid."

were writing down "Stupid Things" on their slates. One of them didn't know how to spell "stupid" and had to ask his neighbor to tell him. "A nice mess his slate will be in, before the trial's over," thought Alice.

One of the jurors, Bill the Lizard, had a pencil that squeaked. The noise got on Alice's nerves to the point that she finally got behind him and sneaked the pencil out of his hand when he wasn't looking. The poor fellow had to write with his finger the rest of the day. But, unfortunately, he made no marks on his slate.

"Herald, read the charges," said the King.

The White Rabbit blew three blasts on the trumpet and then unrolled the parchment scroll and read as follows:

"The Queen of Hearts, she made some tarts, all on a summer day. The Knave of Hearts, he stole those tarts, and took them clean away."

"Consider your verdict," the King loudly

instructed the jury.

"Not yet," the Rabbit interrupted. "There's a great deal to deal with before that."

"Call the first witness," said the King, and the White Rabbit blew three blasts on the trumpet and called out, "First Witness!"

The first witness was the Hatter. He walked in with a teacup in one hand and a piece of bread and butter in the other. "I beg pardon, your Majesty," he began, "for bringing these in, but I hadn't finished my tea when I was sent for."

"You ought to have finished," said the King. "When did you begin?"

The Hatter looked at the March Hare, who had followed him into the court, arm-in-arm with the Dormouse. "Fourteenth of March, I think it was," he said.

"Fifteenth," replied the March Hare.

"Sixteenth," cried the Dormouse.

"Write that down," the King told the jury.

Three Blasts on the Trumpet

Eagerly the jury wrote down all the dates on their slates, added them up, and reduced the answer to dollars and cents.

"Take off your hat," the King told the Hatter.

"It isn't mine," the Hatter stated.

"Stolen!" the King exclaimed, turning to the jury, who instantly made a memo of that fact.

"I keep them to sell," the Hatter explained. "I don't have any of my own. I'm a hatter."

"Let's hear your evidence," said the King, "and don't be nervous, or I'll have you executed on the spot."

This did not seem to encourage the witness at all. He kept shifting from one foot to the other, looking uneasily at the Queen. In his confusion he bit a large piece of his teacup instead of the bread and butter.

Just at that moment Alice realized she was beginning to grow larger again. At first she thought she would leave the court. Then she decided to stay where she was, as long as there was room for her.

"You're squeezing me to death," wailed the Dormouse, who was sitting next to her. "I can hardly breathe."

"I can't help it," Alice said meekly. "I'm growing."

"You've no right to grow here," said the Dormouse.

"Don't talk nonsense," Alice spoke up boldly. "You know you're growing, too."

"Yes, but I grow at a reasonable pace," said the Dormouse, "not in that ridiculous fashion." And he got up very sulkily and walked over to the other side of the court.

All this time the Queen had been staring at the Hatter. Just as the Dormouse crossed the court, she said to one of the officers, "Bring me the list of singers at the last concert."

Hearing this, the wretched Hatter trembled so badly that he shook off his shoes.

"Give your evidence," the King repeated

"I'm a Poor Man, Your Majesty."

angrily, "or I'll have you executed whether you're nervous or not."

"I'm a poor man, your Majesty," the Hatter began in a trembling voice, "and I hadn't begun my tea—and what with the bread and butter getting so thin—and the twinkling of the tea—"

"The twinkling of what?" asked the King.

"It began with the tea," the Hatter replied.

"Of course twinkling begins with a T!" said the King sharply. "Do you take me for a fool?"

"Most things twinkled after that," the Hatter went on, "only the March Hare said—"

"I didn't," the March Hare interrupted.

"He denies it," said the King. "Leave out that part."

The Hatter went on looking anxiously around to see if the Dormouse would deny it, too, but the little fellow denied nothing because he was fast asleep.

"After that," continued the Hatter, "I fixed

some more bread and butter."

"But what did the Dormouse say?" one of the jurors asked.

"I can't remember," mumbled the Hatter.

"You must remember," remarked the King, "or I'll have you beheaded."

"I'm a poor man, your Majesty," began the Hatter, dropping his teacup and bread and butter and going down on one knee.

"You're a very poor speaker," said the King. "If that's all you know about the matter, you may stand down."

"I can't get any lower," said the Hatter. "I'm on the floor, as it is."

"Then you may sit down," the King replied.

"I'd rather finish my tea," said the Hatter, with an anxious look at the Queen, who was reading the list of singers.

"You may go," said the King, and the Hatter rushed out of court without even putting his shoes back on.

"Or I'll Have You Beheaded."

"Call the next witness," said the King.

The next witness was the Duchess's cook. Although she carried a can of pepper in her hand, Alice knew who it was even before she entered the court because people near the door suddenly began sneezing.

"Give your evidence," the King instructed.

"I won't," announced the cook.

The King looked at the White Rabbit, who said in a soft voice, "Your Majesty must cross-examine this witness."

"What are tarts made of?" asked the King in a deep voice.

"Pepper, mostly," said the cook.

"Treacle," replied a sleepy voice behind her.

"Behead that Dormouse!" shrieked the Queen.

"Run him out of this court! Off with his whiskers!"

For a few minutes the whole court was in a state of confusion, getting rid of the Dormouse.

By the time they had settled down again, the cook had disappeared, too.

"Never mind," said the King, greatly relieved. "Call the next witness." Under his breath he told the Queen, "Really, my dear, you must cross-examine the next witness. This whole thing has given me a headache."

Alice watched the White Rabbit as he fumbled over the list, curious to see who the next witness would be. "They haven't got much evidence yet," she thought.

Imagine her surprise when the White Rabbit read out, at the top of his shrill voice, the name "Alice!"

She Tipped Over the Jury Box.

CHAPTER FOURTEEN

Alice's Evidence

"Here," cried Alice, quite forgetting in the flurry of the moment how large she'd grown in the last few minutes. She jumped up in such a hurry that she tipped over the jury box with the hem of her skirt, upsetting all the jurors. They lay sprawled about, squirming every which way, reminding her of the bowl of goldfish she had accidentally upset the week before.

"Oh, I beg your pardon," she exclaimed in dismay and began picking them up as quickly as she could. Somehow she had the vague idea that they must be put back in the jury box at once or they would die.

"The trial cannot proceed," said the King gravely, "until all the jurors are back in their proper places." As he spoke, he glared at Alice.

Alice looked at the jury box and saw that, in her haste, she had put the Lizard in head first, and the poor little thing was waving its tail about wildly, unable to move. Quickly she pulled him out again and set him aright.

As soon as the jury had recovered from the shock of all this, and their slates and pencils had been returned to them, they got to work writing out in great detail the story of their mishap. That was, everyone except the Lizard, who was much too upset to do anything but sit with his mouth open, gazing up at the ceiling of the court.

She Had Put the Lizard in Head First.

"What do you know about this business with the tarts?" the King asked Alice.

"Nothing," said Alice, quite honestly.

"Nothing whatever?" persisted the King, leaning forward and staring hard at her.

"Nothing whatever," said Alice.

"That's very important," the King said to the jury.

The jurors were just beginning to write this down on their slates, when the White Rabbit interrupted. "Unimportant, your Majesty means, of course,"he said in a very respectful tone. Yet at the same time he frowned at the King and made funny faces.

"I meant unimportant, of course," the King said quickly and muttered to himself, "important, unimportant, important, unimportant." It was almost as if he were trying to see which word sounded best.

Some of the jurors wrote down "important" and others "unimportant." Alice could see this, as she was near enough to look at their slates. "Well, it really doesn't matter a bit," she thought to herself.

"Silence!" bellowed the King and read from his book, "Rule forty-two. All persons more than a mile high must leave the court."

Everyone looked at Alice.

"I'm not a mile high," declared Alice.

"Nearly two miles high," added the Queen.

"Well, I refuse to go," said Alice. "Besides, that's not a regular rule. It's one you just invented."

"It's the oldest rule in the book," insisted the King, who slammed his book shut hastily. "Consider your verdict," he instructed the jury in a low trembling voice.

"There's more evidence to come, if it please your Majesty," said the White Rabbit, jumping up in a great hurry. "This paper has just been delivered."

"What's in it?" asked the Queen.

"I Didn't Write It," Said the Knave.

"I haven't opened it yet," said the White Rabbit, "but it seems to be a letter written by the prisoner to—to somebody."

"Unless it was written to nobody," said the King, "which isn't the usual way, you know."

"Who is it addressed to?" inquired one of the jurors.

"It isn't addressed to anyone at all," said the White Rabbit. "In fact, there's nothing written on the outside." He unfolded the paper and added, "It isn't a letter, after all. It's a poem."

"Is it in the prisoner's handwriting?" asked another of the jurors.

"No, it's not," said the White Rabbit, "and that's the strangest thing about it." The jury all looked puzzled.

"He must have imitated somebody else's hand," said the King. At this, the jury brightened up again.

"Please, your Majesty," said the Knave. "I didn't write it, and they can't prove that I did.

There's no name signed at the end."

"If you didn't sign it," said the King, "that only makes the matter worse. You must have meant some mischief, or else you'd have signed your name like an honest man."

Everyone in the courtroom clapped their hands loudly, as they thought that was the first really clever thing the King had said all day.

"That proves his guilt, of course," said the Queen, "so off with—"

"It doesn't prove anything of the sort," said Alice. "Why, you don't even know what the poem is about."

"Read it," ordered the King.

There was dead silence in the court, as the White Rabbit began to read:

"They told me you had been to her,
    And mentioned me to him;
She gave me a good character,

Everyone Clapped Loudly.

But said I could not swim.

He sent them word I had not gone
    We knew it to be true;
If she should push the matter on,
    What would become of you?

I gave her one, they gave him two.
    You gave us three or more;
They all returned from him to you,
    Though they were mine before.

If I or she should chance to be
    Involved in this affair,
He trusts to you to set them free,
    Exactly as we were.

My notion was that you had been
    Before she had this fit
An obstacle that came between
    Him, and ourselves, and it.

Don't let him know she liked them best,
   For this must ever be
A secret kept from all the rest,
   Between yourself and me."

"That's the most important piece of evidence we've heard yet," said the King.

"I don't believe there's an atom of meaning in it," replied Alice. At this point she had grown so large that she wasn't afraid of interrupting the King.

"If there's no meaning in it," said the King, "that saves us a lot of trouble because we won't need to find any. And yet I don't know," he went on, spreading out the paper on his knee and reading the verses. "I seem to see some meaning in it, after all—said I could not swim—You can't swim, can you?" he asked the Knave.

The Knave shook his head sadly, "Do I look like it?" Being made of cardboard, he really did

"Never!" Cried the Queen.

not look like it.

The King went on muttering over the verses, "'We knew it to be true'—that's the jury, of course—'if she should push the matter on'—that must be the Queen—'What would become of you?'—What indeed!—'I gave her one, they gave him two'—Why, that must be what he did with the tarts."

"But it goes on 'they all returned from him to you',", said Alice.

"Why, there they are," said the King triumphantly, pointing to the tarts on the table. "Nothing can be clearer than that. Then again—'before she had this fit'—you never had fits,—my dear, did you?" he asked the Queen.

"Never!" cried the Queen, throwing an inkstand at the Lizard as she spoke. The unfortunate little Bill had stopped writing on his slate with one finger, as he found it made no mark. Immediately he began using the ink that was trickling down his face.

"Then the words don't fit you," said the King, looking around the court with a smile. There was dead silence.

"It's a pun," the King added angrily and everybody laughed. "Let the jury consider their verdict."

"No, no," said the Queen. "Sentence first—verdict afterwards."

"Stuff and nonsense," cried Alice loudly. "The idea of having the sentence first."

"Hold your tongue!" yelled the Queen, turning purple.

"I won't," said Alice defiantly.

"Off with her head," the Queen shouted, but nobody moved.

"I'm not afraid of you," said Alice, who had grown to her full size by this time. "You're nothing but a pack of cards."

Suddenly the whole pack rose up in the air and came flying down upon her. Screaming, Alice tried to fight them off and found herself

"You're Nothing But a Pack of Cards."

lying on the river bank with her head in the lap of her sister who was gently brushing away some dead leaves that had fluttered down from the trees upon her face.

"Wake up, Alice, dear," said her sister. "Why, what a long sleep you've had."

"Oh, I've had the most curious dream," replied Alice, and she told her sister all her strange adventures that you have been reading about.

When she had finished her story, her sister kissed her and said, "It was a curious dream certainly, but now you must go and get your tea. It's getting late."

So Alice got up and ran off, thinking while she ran just what a wonderful dream it had been. Somehow she knew, down deep in her heart, she'd remember it all her life.